Richard O. Beard, Newton H. Winchell

Hand-book of Minneapolis

prepared for the thirty-second annual meeting of the American

association for the advancement of science, held in Minneapolis, Minn.,

Aug. 15-22, 1883

Richard O. Beard, Newton H. Winchell

Hand-book of Minneapolis
prepared for the thirty-second annual meeting of the American association for the
advancement of science, held in Minneapolis, Minn., Aug. 15-22, 1883

ISBN/EAN: 9783337288525

Printed in Europe, USA, Canada, Australia, Japan

Cover: Foto ©Andreas Hilbeck / pixelio.de

More available books at **www.hansebooks.com**

OF

MINNEAPOLIS,

PREPARED FOR THE THIRTY-SECOND ANNUAL MEETING
OF THE

AMERICAN ASSOCIATION FOR THE
ADVANCEMENT OF SCIENCE,

HELD IN

VIEW OF FORT SNELLING.

TABLE OF CONTENTS.

PREFACE.

Previous to the inception of this volume no concise history, either of the City of Minneapolis or of the State of Minnesota, had ever been attempted. The materials at hand for its preparation were, therefore, of a very fragmentary nature, and have with difficulty been fitted together, in the effort to hastily frame a continuous record. Judging that the history of a large city is inseparable, particularly in its early years, from that of the commonwealth of which it forms so important a part, its designers have intended that the first thirty pages of the volume should serve as an appropriate introduction to the principal and more specific portion of the work. The one is simply the natural background on which the separate features of the other may be more distinctly traced. The Author, in concluding his work, desires to record his obligations to Prof. N. H. Winchell, *of the State Geological Survey*, for his invaluable assistance in the collection and arrangement of geological and physical facts. To the different writers whose works he has consulted, and from whose stores of information he has freely drawn, he would acknowledge his indebtedness, *en masse*.

Minneapolis, Minnesota, August 7, 1883.

Tribune Job Dep't. Print.

SUSPENSION BRIDGE.

THE

History of Minnesota,

FROM 1640 TO 1883.

PRE-TERRITORIAL HISTORY. A. D. 1640-1849.

LTHOUGH nearly two centuries and a half have elapsed since a white man's foot first trod "The Land of the Dakotahs," Minnesota has but thirty-four years of state and territorial history, and for only twenty years have the settlers held undisputed possession of the soil. The recognition of its natural advantages was long delayed and the tides of immigration long held in check by the dreaded presence of uncivilized Indian tribes, whose constant irruptions threatened the peace and safety of every homestead planted upon the border. Very slowly the attractions of the country overcame the settlers' fear of the savages, as step by step the latter relinquished their hold upon their old-time possessions, until, at last, in 1862 — by the massacre of hundreds of human beings —they forfeited their last title to the land.

TRAVEL AND EXPLORATION.

THE PRE-TERRITORIAL HISTORY of Minnesota, a record, for the most part, of travel and exploration, begins with the year 1640.

At this period, the south and southwest portions of the present state were occupied by bands of Ioways, Ottoes, Cheyennes and Omahaws; the whole central region west and northwest of Mille Lacs by the Dakotahs or Sioux; and the northeast by the Assiniboines, a separated family of the Dakotahs.

FRENCH EXPLORERS.

The neighboring territory being in the hands of France, French explorers were naturally the first to be tempted to the discovery of the New West. Accordingly, we learn that in 1640 a man named Nicolet visited the

Dakotahs and Assiniboines, and that in 1659 Groselliers and Radisson, two commercial agents, crossed Lake Superior and wintered with a band of Dakotahs in the vicinity of Mille Lacs.

In 1661, Rene Menard, traveling by way of the Wisconsin river, was doubtless the first to discover the upper Mississippi, but his loss, or death by violence, in the forests of the Black river, obscured the evidence of the fact.

Claude Allouez, a Jesuit Father, visited the Minnesota shores of Lake Superior in 1665, and first reported the native name of the great river as "Messipi."

Daniel Greysolon Du Luth was the actual discoverer of Minnesota, in the year 1679. He entered the St. Louis river from Lake Superior with a party of eight men, and journeyed to a "great village of the Sioux," named Kathio, near Red Lake or Lake of the Woods, where he formally set up the arms of the King of France. He established the first trading posts in Minnesota, and traveling down the St. Croix river reached the Mississippi, where he met Hennepin ascending the river with a band of Dakotah Indians.

Louis Hennepin, who first made the *ascent* of the Mississippi, was a Franciscan priest of the Recollect order, a native of the Netherlands. Having accompanied La Salle's expedition to the Illinois river, he left the latter, in company with two men, for the purpose of exploring the Upper Mississippi. He ascended the river by boat to within a short distance of the great falls, whence he journeyed with the Dakotah Indians to Mille Lacs. Later he discovered and named the falls after St. Anthony of Padua.

In 1683 Nicholas Perrot started a trading post in the neighborhood of Lake Pepin, which he revisited in 1688, when he officially laid claim to the country in the name of the French King.

In 1695 Le Sueur arrived at Lake Pepin, above which he established another trading post. Five years later he passed the Minnesota river in search of copper, and built Fort L'Huillier on the Blue Earth river.

During the early part of the eighteenth century, the constant warfare between the Indian tribes was repeatedly aggravated, and the traders suffered much in consequence. In 1755, the war between Great Britain and France engaged the tribes in its conflicting interests, and added the horrors of savage warfare to the strife of civilized nations.

BRITISH POSSESSIONS IN MINNESOTA.

At its close France ceded all that part of Minnesota east of a line drawn from the international boundary to the head of the Mississippi, and thence along the course of that river, to Great Britain; retaining the territory west of this line in her own possession, under the title of the province of *Louisiane*, which extended to the 49th parallel.

In 1766 Jonathan Carver, an Englishman, visited Lake Pepin and St. Anthony's Falls. Thirty miles below the latter he discovered a large cave which took his name but has since become concealed or destroyed. He went up the Minnesota River as far as the Cottonwood, where he stayed several months.

THE REVOLUTIONARY WAR.

"The War of the Revolution," says Professor Winchell,* "which left the east bank of the Mississippi in the possession of the United States and the west bank in the possession of the French, operated not only to terminate English and French exploration, but to retard that of the United States. It was not till after the cession of Louisiana by France that the Government instituted measures for the exploration of the unknown country west of the Mississippi."

The year 1783 witnessed the formation of the Northwest Fur Co., which proved a formidable rival for many years to the Hudson Bay Company Its geographer, Mr. David Thompson, crossed the limits of the present State in 1798 from the Red river of the North to Lake Superior.

THE CESSION OF LOUISIANA.

In 1804 the cession of Louisiana by France took place and included the whole of Minnesota west of the Mississippi. During the following year, Lieutenant Z. M. Pike, with a company of soldiers, was despatched to the upper Mississippi country by the United States government to enforce the recognition of United States' authority upon the traders, to make treaties with the tribes, and to determine the location of military posts. He visited several trading establishments, and made a report of a large part of the country previously unknown save to the *couriers des bois* of the fur companies. Returning he encamped on the island at the junction of the Minnesota and Mississippi rivers, and while there obtained from the Dakotahs a grant of land extending nine miles on either side of the Mississippi from below the junction of the rivers to the Falls of St. Anthony.

At the outbreak of the War of 1812 many American trading posts in Minnesota were surprised and taken by the British soldiers and traders in alliance with the Indians. At its conclusion, the United States made a treaty of peace with the Dakotahs, and American traders soon after appeared in Minnesota in larger numbers.

The year 1818 was marked by a fiercer outbreak than usual between the Ojibways and Dakotahs.

*Historical sketch of Explorations and Surveys of Minnesota, by Prof. N. H. Winchell.

A colony of English and Swiss, founded by the Earl of Selkirk about 1812, near Pembina, in the northwest corner of the State, which had struggled through a precarious existence, imperilled by Indian treachery, by flood and famine, and by the jealousies of the rival fur companies, was found to be encroaching upon the United States territory and was restrained by order of the government.

THE ERECTION OF FORT SNELLING.

In 1819 the authorities ordered the erection of a military post at the mouth of the Minnesota, and Lieut. Col. Leavenworth, with ninety-eight officers and men, was despatched to that point. On September 20th, 1820, the corner-stone of Fort Snelling was laid, and pending its completion the force encamped, opposite Mendota, near to an old post known as the Baker trading house. Lieut. Col. Leavenworth was relieved by Colonel Snelling before the fort was ready for occupation. Mrs. Snelling accompanied her husband, and a few days after her arrival gave birth to the first white child born in Minnesota. She and other officers' wives were the first ladies to winter in the State.

In 1823 the first steamboat, the "Virginia," navigated the Upper Mississippi, passing up to Mendota. During the year, by order of the Government, Major S. H. Long with a scientific corps, including Prof. William Keating, of Pennsylvania University, who made a report of the expedition, explored the Minnesota river and fixed the United States north boundary line. J. C. Beltrami, an Italian political exile who had accompanied the expedition, having some difficulty with Major Long, severed himself from the force at Pembina, and moving southeastward discovered the Julian sources of the Mississippi.

THE FIRST SETTLERS.

About this time a number of Swiss settlers, driven southeast from the Selkirk settlement by flood and famine, settled near the subsequent sites of St. Anthony and St. Paul. They were practically the first settlers of Minnesota.

In 1827 a brief but bloody strife aggravated the perpetual warfare of the Ojibway and Dakotah tribes. Several mission stations, notably at Lake Harriet and Lac qui Parle, were established by Presbyterian and independent missionaries in the years following 1829, but considering the means and labor expended upon the work they made but a slight impression upon the native tribes.

In 1832 Minnesota shared to some extent in the excitement occasioned by the Black Hawk war. During this year Mr. H. R. Schoolcraft traced the Mississippi river to its source in Lake Itasca, of which Mr. Schoolcraft claimed to be the discoverer, notwithstanding the fact that a letter from Mr. Wm. Morrison to "The Historical Society of Minnesota" gives an account of a visit made there in 1804.

Two years later the inhabitants presented a petition to Congress praying that Minnesota be organized as a territory or attached to that of Michigan, and the latter alternative was temporarily chosen.

The year 1836 is memorable for the arrival at Fort Snelling of Jean M. Nicollet, who made the most complete exploration of the Mississippi, finally determined its sources, and subsequently explored the whole interior of the present State.

Treaties were made by Governor Dodge, in 1837, with the Ojibways and Dakotahs, by which the pine forests of the St. Croix and its tributaries and all lands east of the Mississippi were ceded to the United States. A portion of these lands between St. Paul and Ft. Snelling was chosen for a military reservation from which certain settlers, who had established themselves in the meantime upon them, were necessarily removed.

THE BIRTH OF CITIES.

Upon a portion of the present site of the city of Stillwater a claim was made in 1840, and lumber was rafted down the St. Croix; three years later a more extended settlement was formed and a saw-mill built at the same point, ultimately determining the future of the place.

The first mill built in Minnesota, outside of the government military reservation, was erected five miles northeast of St. Paul, in 1844.

The city of St. Paul had its beginnings in the years between 1840 and 1847. Liquor-selling was its earliest traffic, to the misfortune alike of whites and savages. A rum-shop was first opened, upon the site of the present principal steamboat landing, by a Frenchman called Parant, whose peculiar appearance gave to the place the euphonious name of "Pig-Eye." A little later a Mankato merchant settled near the same spot and erected the first store, which was quickly followed by other small trading shops. As much as four years afterward (1844) it is said that "the site of St. Paul was chiefly occupied by a few shanties," principally for the sale of rum to the soldiers and Indians. Not until 1847 was the first common school in Minnesota established at St. Paul, under care of Miss H. E. Bishop.

In the next year the Winnebagoes very unwillingly fulfilled a treaty made with the government for their removal from Iowa to the region lying between the Sank, Long Prairie and Crow Wing rivers in Minnesota.

THE ORGANIZATION OF THE TERRITORY.

The principal inhabitants brought to bear, at this time, all the influence they possessed, at Washington, to secure a territorial organization, and on March 3, 1849, shortly after the admission of Wisconsin to the Union, the Territory of Minnesota was organized by act of Congress, and the city of St. Paul was named as the capital.

TERRITORIAL HISTORY.—A. D., 1849—1858.

A T the time of the organization of Minnesota Territory the whole of the country west of the Mississippi, from Lake Itasca to the southern boundary, was still in possession of the Indians, and, with the exception of a few trading posts, isolated settlements, and mission stations, was practically unsettled by the whites. The whole population of the Territory, as determined by the first territorial census of 1849, numbered only 4,680.

THE INDIAN TRIBES

within its borders, little influenced by missionary effort, and depraved by drink, had been and still were constantly engaged in petty warfare with each other, and in occasional robbery and murder of the white settlers. Undeterred either by treaties or military severity, these barbarities appeared to increase yearly in number, a fact not unnaturally accounted for, perhaps, by the Indian's growing jealousy of the white man's encroachment upon his ancient domain. An attempt, made at this time, to obtain from them a cession of the lands west of the Mississippi, proved inconclusive, having no other result than the purchase of Lake Pepin. Hardly had the territory been organized when renewed hostilities were opened between the Ojibways and Dakotahs.

THE PRINCIPAL CITIES

of Minnesota were still in embryo: Minneapolis, as yet, was not; St. Anthony held hardly the germ of its future: Stillwater was in its early, formative stages; and even St. Paul was yet little more than a group of small frame tenements, whiskey shops and log cabins. The appointment of the latter city as the Capital of the Territory quickly brought people to the place, and within a year it held 250 to 300 inhabitants.

The first Minnesota newspaper was started at once, under title of "The Pioneer," by James M. Goodhue. Alexander Ramsey, the first Governor of the Territory, H. H. Sibley, its first delegate to Congress, and H. M. Rice, first United States senator after the admission of Minnesota to the Union, were among the men most instrumental in shaping the interests of the new Territory.

TERRITORIAL GOVERNMENT.

By its permanent organization it was divided into seven council districts, and an election for one delegate to Congress, nine councillors and eighteen representatives was ordered. The first courts were convened at Stillwater, St. Anthony and Mendota, and the first Legislative Assembly created nine counties. During this year the site of a new military post was selected near Pembina. Steam navigation of the Minnesota river was commenced. The historical society was duly incorporated and opened its first session at St. Paul in January, 1850. In 1851 the penitentiary was placed at Stillwater, and an act passed the Legislature for the creation of the University of Minnesota, to be situated in the neighborhood of the Falls of St. Anthony. A treaty was made with the Dakotahs by which the Territory upon the west side of the Mississippi, and in the valley of the Minnesota river, was opened to immigration. During this winter the Ojibways suffered severely from famine and disease.

In 1852 Hennepin county was created, and in the year following eleven counties were formed in the Territory west of the Mississippi. At this legislative session a liquor bill, similar to that known as the "Maine Law," passed the Legislature and was approved by the voice of the people, but was declared unconstitutional by the courts at its first application.

At the beginning of President Pierce's administration, W. A. Gorman succeeded Alexander Ramsey as Governor of Minnesota Territory. A supposed fraud charged upon the late Governor and others, in the transfer of funds to the Dakotahs, was successfully disproved before a United States commission appointed to investigate the same. During this year the Dakotahs commenced their northward march to the region of the upper Minnesota, and a treaty was made by Governor Gorman with the Winnebagoes providing for their removal to another reservation.

In 1854 the Legislative Assembly passed an act for the incorporation of the Minnesota & Northwestern railroad. In the same year Congress voted a land grant to the Territory of Minnesota for purposes of railway construction. A month later Mr. Washburne, of Illinois, stated in Congress that certain clauses in this land-grant bill had been altered subsequent to its engrossment, and, acting upon this plea, the House repealed the bill. The Minnesota & Northwestern railroad, previously chartered, claimed that Congress had no power to repeal the act. A complaint was brought against the company in the United States district court, charging that it had cut and removed certain trees from United States property in Goodhue county. Judge Welch, presiding, gave a decision for the railroad company; the supreme court of Minnesota confirmed his decision; and the supreme court of the United States, to which it was carried, discontinued the case,

in 1850, on motion of the attorney-general.   The discussion concerning
the charter of the Minnesota & Northwestern railroad was renewed in 1855.
The United States Senate rejected the House bill annulling the charter, and
it was subsequently amended twice by the Minnesota Assembly.

In 1857 considerable popular excitement was created by an abortive
attempt to remove the seat of government from St. Paul to St. Peter.
During this year the community was shocked and disturbed by the news
of an outrage committed by a band of outlawed Indians in the southwest
corner of the Territory, resulting in the murder of eighteen persons and the
kidnapping of four women, two of whom were afterwards killed and two
rescued.   A general feeling of insecurity naturally followed every fresh
evidence of lawlessness on the part of the Indians; a feeling which the
terrible sequel of 1862 amply justified.

ADMISSION TO THE UNION.

The United States Senate, on February 23, 1857, passed an act author-
izing the people of the Territory to frame a constitution with a view to the
immediate admission of Minnesota to the Union.   At the same session of
Congress it was voted to grant to Minnesota certain lands, in alternate
sections, for purposes of railroad construction.   The Governor called an
extra session of the Legislative Assembly to adopt measures necessary in
the premises.   The land-grant was disposed of and an election ordered for
the choice of delegates to a convention charged with drafting the constitution.   The election was held, and after a rupture continued for several
weeks between the two political parties, each claiming a rightful majority,
a form of constitution was jointly agreed upon.   At the following October
election this constitution was almost unanimously adopted by the people.
On January 29, 1858, an act providing for the admission of Minnesota
into the Union was introduced in the United States Senate by Mr. Douglas.
On April 7th, following, the bill passed the Senate, soon obtained the con-
currence of the Lower House, and receiving the signature of the President
on May 11, 1858, Minnesota was henceforth one of the United States of
America.

STATE HISTORY, 1858—1883.

HE early years of Minnesota's State History were times of great financial embarrassment to the new commonwealth in common with the country at large, and this embarrassment was greatly deepened by unfortunate legislation in aid of railroad construction.

THE STATE RAILROAD BONDS.

The land grant of 4,500,000 acres made by Congress for the construction of a system of railroads was distributed to several chartered railway corporations, who proved unable to prosecute the required work. To meet the emergency, an act passed the Legislature in 1858 submitting an amendment to the people providing for the issue of $5,000,000 of State Railroad Bonds to these chartered roads as a public loan, conditioned upon partial construction to a stated extent. Despite the active exertions of an intelligent opposing party the amendment was carried by a large majority.

The railroads again failed to perform the required work, and $2,000,000 worth of bonds were issued before a rail was laid.

The Hon. H. H. Sibley, first Governor of the State, found his term of office, as did many of his successors, much embarrassed by these State loans.

To anticipate, briefly, the history of this unfortunate question:—The people, in 1860, had so far realized their mistake, that they voted an amendment to the constitution expunging the foregoing, and prohibiting the further issuance of the State Railroad Bonds. Provision for the payment of those already issued was continually delayed and their non-redemption remained for twenty-three years a perpetual stumbling-block in the way of State legislators and executive, and a standing injury to the credit of the commonwealth. In 1881, after much abortive legislation and largely through the persistent influence of Governor John S. Pillsbury and others, the State Legislature passed an act providing for the acceptance of terms of settlement proposed by the bondholders and the cancellation of outstanding bonds. Thereby the State was relieved of an impending accusation of repudiatory tendencies, and freed from the onus of a too long threatened disgrace.

EDUCATIONAL INTERESTS.

To return to the regular course of events,—in 1858 the Legislature voted the establishment of three State Normal Schools, to be situated at Winona, St. Cloud and Mankato. In 1859 Alexander Ramsey was elected Governor to succeed the Hon. H. H. Sibley. During his first term of office the Legislature passed a bill regulating the State University, and another uniting the two offices of Chancellor of the University and Superintendent of Public Instruction, which, at a subsequent session, were again separated. Following the recommendations of Governor Ramsey's annual message, the Legislature of 1861 initiated a series of legislative acts favorably affecting the educational interests of the State, and inaugurated a school land policy, which has been amply justified by its results.

THE WAR OF THE REBELLION.

At the outbreak of the Civil War Governor Ramsey was in Washington, and after the fall of Sumter was the first governor to offer to the President the military services of his State. The citizens of Minnesota quickly responded to the call for volunteers, and the first regiment was promptly enrolled and forwarded to Washington. During the entire war the State furnished eleven infantry regiments, four regiments of cavalry, one of heavy artillery, three batteries, and two companies of sharpshooters, which served efficiently in the different divisions of the army during the greater period of the war. The first Minnesota regiment was attached to the Army of the Potomac and was actively engaged in twenty-one battles. It mustered throughout 1,440 men, of which number less than one-third returned "to tell the story."

THE SIOUX MASSACRE.

Whilst the interests of the whole country were most painfully centered in the south, there occurred in the valley of the Minnesota an event which, for the time, eclipsed even the horrors of the Civil war,—THE SIOUX MASSACRE OF 1862. Many and remote are the causes which have been assigned to this fearful outbreak of the Sioux Indians, but it is probable that no one cause will sufficiently account for the irruption, still less for the violence and suddenness of its character. A growing spirit of discontent had doubtless been fostered for a long period among the tribes, manifesting itself by occasional isolated atrocity. The delay experienced in the receipt of government annuities, the poor quality and deficient quantity of their food, their misunderstandings with the traders, the gradual advance of the whites upon the borders of the reservation, their dislike of the missionaries among them, and the recognized absence from the State of large numbers of men engaged in the war, have all been cited as causative influences, and each may have helped to aggravate the natural propensity for outrage. The immediate occasion for executing their fearful purpose appears to have been the determination of the tribe to protect a small number of young warriors from the consequences of the murder of a certain white family, committed whilst the savages were under the influence of alcohol. However this may be, it is known that on the morning of August 18, 1862, a large body of Indians attacked the Lower Agency and promiscuously slaughtered the inmates, with the exception of one man, George H. Spencer, and a few women and children; that, proceeding to the Upper Agency, they killed a large number of men, allowing the missionaries, however, with their families and a few others, to escape; and, that then scattering themselves along the frontier for nearly two hundred miles, they indiscriminately slew every white settler within reach of their weapons. Young women and children were alone spared, only to become prisoners and in many cases to suffer brutal outrage at the hands of their captors. It is estimated that, in all, some eight hundred persons were massacred. Forts Ridgley and Abercrombie and the town of New Ulm were attacked, but successfully defended with some loss of life. The alarm quickly spread and thousands of frightened settlers flocked the roads to the larger towns. Immediate steps were taken by the governor and others to stay the massacre and punish its authors. Col. H. H. Sibley was put at the head of a force of four hundred men, who, owing to the previous drain upon the State for men, arms and ammunition, were difficult to gather and scantily equipped. These hastily prepared troops advanced to the Lower Agency as rapidly as possible, where a party of them, whilst engaged in burying the victims of the massacre, were attacked by the Dakotahs. The latter were beaten back after a brief fight, and three days later were defeated with considerable loss. They delivered up the captives in their hands, surrendered themselves prisoners, and were duly tried. Over three hundred were found guilty of participation in the massacre and condemned to be hung, but the sentence was suspended by order of the President, and only thirty-eight were eventually executed. The remainder were imprisoned at Davenport, Iowa, for over a year, where many died from disease; the survivors were ultimately conveyed to a reservation on the upper Missouri river. In the following year the Government organized and despatched an efficient force to capture and punish those who had escaped from the hands of Colonel Sibley and his men.

DOMESTIC AFFAIRS.

Immigration to Minnesota was materially checked by the massacre of 1862, and some time elapsed before it recovered from its effects. In 1862 Governor Ramsey was re-elected, but the year following he was chosen United States senator and resigned the governorship to take his seat in the Senate. Lieutenant Governor Swift filled the office until the succession of Stephen Miller, in 1864. He was followed by Wm. R. Marshall, in 1866, who served for two terms. In 1870 Horace Austin succeeded to the office and was re-elected in 1872.

In 1874 C. K. Davis was inaugurated Governor. During his term an important test case, concerning the power of the state to determine railway rates, was carried to the supreme court of the United States, which rendered the note-worthy decision that the state power to regulate rates was not limited by the charter of the railway company.

In 1875 the people voted amendments to the constitution relating to terms of office, judicial districts, investment of funds from the sale of school lands, and the permission of women to vote for school officers. During this year and the preceding the farming communities suffered from the depredations of the locust or grasshopper.

In 1876 John S. Pillsbury was chosen Governor of the State and was re-elected in 1877 and 1879. At the former of these elections the people approved amendments to the constitution concerning the canvassing of election returns, the election and term of senators and representatives, biennial sessions of the Legislature, and the prohibition of the use of State funds for sectarian schools. In 1881 the first biennial session of the Legislature was held.

In January, 1882, Lucius F. Hubbard succeeded John S. Pillsbury as Governor of the State. With the exception of the first State Governor, Gen. H. H. Sibley, all the Governors of the State have been republican in politics. The later years of Minnesota's State history have been an era of unbroken and almost unexampled prosperity, marked by a rapid increase of population, a corresponding growth in trade, manufacture and the development of natural products, and a wide extension of the railway service. For a comparative estimate, showing the progress of the State in each of these directions, the reader is referred to the tables on pages 32–38.

PHYSICAL FEATURES, GEOLOGY AND MINERALOGY OF MINNESOTA.

SITUATION, BOUNDARIES, AND AREA OF THE STATE.

MINNESOTA occupies nearly the geographical centre of the North American continent, being about 1000 miles from the Atlantic ocean and the Gulf of Mexico, and about 1400 miles from the Arctic sea and Pacific ocean.

On the north this State is bounded by the British provinces of Manitoba, Kewatin, and Ontario, the international boundary line, between the Red river of the North and the Lake of the Woods, being the 49th parallel. The continuation of this boundary thence to Lake Superior is made up of water-courses and lakes. It has an east-southeasterly course, and consists of the Lake of the Woods, Rainy river and lake, and a succession of small lakes, extending by the south side of the area marked on the map as Hunter's Island, to Saganago and Gunflint lakes, and to the divide between the waters of Hudson bay and those of Lake Superior; beyond which it passes through a further series of lakes at the head of Arrow and Pigeon rivers, and down the latter river to Pigeon Point at its mouth, on the northeast shore of Lake Superior, which is the most eastern point of Minnesota.

On the east, Minnesota is bounded by Lake Superior and Wisconsin, being divided from Wisconsin by the Saint Croix and Mississippi rivers. On the south it is bounded by Iowa at the parallel of 43° 30 : and on the west by Dakota, from which it is separated in part by Big Stone Lake, Lake Traverse, and the Red river of the North.

The length of Minnesota from north to south is 380 miles, the extreme length 408, for a tract of about 150 square miles, extending 28 miles north of the 49th parallel, on the west side of the Lake of the Woods, belongs to this State. This point is the most northerly portion of the United States, excepting Alaska. The extreme width of Minnesota, from east to west, measured from Pigeon Point to the Red river is about 350 miles, and its width at the narrowest part, from the St. Croix river west to Dakota is 180 miles. The eastern and western limits of the State are approximately in longitude 90° and 97° west from Greenwich, or 13° and 20° west from Washington.

The area of Minnesota, compiled from the maps of the governmental surveys, by Hon. H. H. Young, Secretary of the Board of Immigration, is in total 84,286 square miles; the land area being 78,649 square miles, or 50,335,367 acres, and the water area, not including any portion of Lake Superior, 5,637 square miles.

RIVERS AND LAKES.

The waters of the State all find their way to the Atlantic ocean, but they reach that level through three of the cardinal points of the compass— north, east and south. The water area of Minnesota is greater than that of any other other State or Territory of the Union, averaging one square mile of water to every fifteen of land. This unequaled water supply leaves the State by the valleys of seven different courses, namely, the Mississippi, the Saint Louis river and Lake Superior, the Red river of the North, the Rainy river, the Des Moines river, the Rock river, and the Cedar river.

The Mississippi river system is by far the largest and most important. It is the only one that crosses the entire State. Its approximate area is 45,566 square miles. The river runs almost exclusively on the surface of the drift to the Falls of St. Anthony; and from there till it leaves the State, and even till it enters the Gulf of Mexico, it runs in an old rocky valley excavated in pre-glacial times. All its tributaries, also, below the Falls of St. Anthony enter it through similar deep-cut gorges. The upper tributaries of this river, however, are post-glacial, and have excavated their valleys but little within the drift sheet. Itasca lake, the head of the Mississippi, is about 1500 feet above the level of the sea. Where the river leaves the State, at its southeast corner, it is only 620 feet above the sea level.

The system of the Red river of the North rises in the same rolling drift region as the Mississippi, at a point about twelve miles west of Itasca lake, at an elevation of 1600 feet above the ocean, and leaves the State, after a circuitous route, with an elevation of 767 feet. The entire area drained by the Red river in Minnesota is heavily covered with northern drift. After leaving the rolling morainic regions of Becker and Otter Tail counties, it passes through the fertile *Red river valley,* which in its flatness and monotony, no less than its area, resembles the northern steppes of Russia and Siberia, with which also it seems to have had an analogous region. The aggregate area of the State included in this basin is 15,107 square miles. The river is navigated by steamboats as far north as Moorhead and Fargo. The flat portion of this basin is prairie; but its northern part, which extends far to the east, embracing Red lake and its tributaries, includes a large area that is timbered.

The Rainy river system has an approximate area, in Minnesota, of 10,330 square miles. It extends along the international boundary from the water-divide to the Lake of the Woods. Its waters are derived from the lakes of a region characterized by many and extensive exposures of rock, as far as to the west end of Rainy lake. To the west of that there are several tributaries from the south which rise in the northern sweep of the belt of morainic hills, and in the flat marshy tract south of Rainy river, which flow upon the surface of the drift-sheet, and very rarely come in contact with the underlying rock. Its area in the State is smaller than that of the Red river of the North, but the annual discharge of water is apparently about double that from the Red river valley. It receives waters from land more than two thousand feet above the ocean, and where it leaves the State it has an altitude, in the Lake of the Woods, of 1042 feet. (Canadian Pacific railway survey).

The Saint Louis river and Lake Superior drainage system includes 8,552 square miles, not including any portion of Lake Superior itself. It occupies the most elevated portion of the State. Its waters descend from over 2000 feet above the sea to 602 feet, the level of Lake Superior. This lake has a mean depth of 1000 feet.

The Des Moines river in Minnesota runs along the northeast side of the Coteau des Prairies, from which it receives numerous small tributaries, and carries off the surface waters from an area of prairie amounting to about 1940 square miles in this State. As this water finally reaches the Mississippi, it might perhaps with propriety be embraced in the drainage system of that river.

The Rock river system, which is tributary to the Missouri river through the Big Sioux, includes about 1702 square miles. This system is confined to the southwesterly slopes of the Coteau des Prairies, the surface of which is smooth and treeless.

The Cedar river system is also connected with the Mississippi in Iowa; is the smallest drainage area of the State, embracing but 1089 square miles of prairie situated mostly in Freeborn and Mower counties.

The number of *lakes* in Minnesota, exceeding 40 rods in diameter, is estimated at ten thousand, and the State atlas shows 2500 which are a half mile or more in length. Rainy lake on the northern border has an area of about 150 square miles, and the Lake of the Woods of about 600 square miles. The largest lake entirely within the limits of Minnesota is Red Lake, which has an approximate area of 340 square miles. Other lakes in Minnesota, next to Red lake in magnitude, are Mille Lacs, nearly 200 square miles in extent; Leech lake, 194 square miles; Lake Winnibigoshish, 78 square miles; Vermilion lake, 63 square miles; Cass lake, 32; and Lake Minnetonka, 24 square miles.*

*Report of Mr. Henry Gannett, geographer of the United States tenth census, 1880.

ALTITUDES AND CONTOUR.

The topographic features of the western three-quarters of Minnesota may be described, in brief, as a moderately undulating, sometimes nearly flat, sometimes hilly expanse, gradually descending from the Coteau des Prairies and the Leaf hills, which lie between 1500 and 2000 feet above the sea. to half that height, or from 800 to 1000 feet above the sea level, in the long flat basin of the Red river valley, and along the valley of the Mississippi, from Minneapolis to Saint Cloud.

The exceptions to this general contour are the southeast part of the State, where the Mississippi and its tributaries are enclosed by bluffs from 200 to 600 feet high, and the northwest shore of Lake Superior, with the country lying to the north of it and to the east of Vermilion lake. In this northwest part of the State, a bold rocky highland rises 400 to 800 feet above Lake Superior, within from one to five miles from its shore-line all along the distance of 150 miles from Duluth to Pigeon point; while further north are many hill-ranges, 200 to 500 feet high, trending from northeast to southwest, or from east to west. The most jagged of these lines of rugged peaks and rock ridges lying near the shore of Lake Superior is called the Sawteeth mountains, which rise from 900 to 1400 feet above the lake and 1500 to 2000 feet above the sea. A second range of hills, rising from the more elevated region halfway between the lake and the north boundary, is called the Mesabi range, and rises south of Vermilion lake and eastward, as stated by Prof. N. H. Winchell, to a height of 1800 to 2200 feet above the sea, this being the highest land in Minnesota. The average elevation of the entire State is probably not far from 1275 feet above the sea.

FOREST AND PRAIRIE.

Minnesota has about 52,200 square miles of forest. and about 31,800 square miles of prarie. including in each the water-areas adjacent to or embraced within them. Forest covers approximately the northeastern two-thirds of the State, while about one-third, lying at the south and southeast and reaching in the Red river valley to the international boundary is prairie. Thin belts and isolated patches of heavy timber are found in several of the prairie counties and along most of the river valleys. Likewise within the heavily timbered portions of the State are found small areas of prairie, or meadow land, especially along the Mississippi from Minneapolis and Anoka to Brainerd. Large areas of timbered lands have been desolated by fire, and although a young growth of trees is rapidly restocking them with forest, they are not now properly regarded as timbered, and therefore they are not taken into account.

The forests of northern Minnesota are largely coniferous, including the white pine, red or "Norway" pine, the Banksian or "jack" pine, black and white spruce, balsam fir, tamarack, arbor vitae, and, in small quantities, red cedar. The deciduous forest consists principally of various species of oak, elm, bass, poplar, maple and ash. Beech and chestnut are not native to the State, but the black walnut and the Kentucky coffee-tree are found as far north as the valley of the Minnesota and Cannon rivers. The white pine is common through the northern part of the State, excepting west of the meridian of Red Lake and Lake of the Woods. It prefers somewhat clayey soil. Occasionally it forms a majestic forest without intermixture of other large trees, but is oftener associated with maple, elm, bass, oak, ash and other deciduous species. It is frequent along the north side of Lake Superior, but forms no extensive forest on the immediate shore. This is the largest and most useful of the native trees, growing from eighty to one hundred and fifty feet in height, and from three to six feet in diameter. The southwestern limit of the pineries extends from the north edge of Chisago county, westerly through Kanabec and Mille Lacs counties, the northeast corner of Benton county, Morrison county and the northeastern part of Todd county, to Pine lakes, Frazee City and the White Earth reservation. Southeastward of this limit it occurs, rarely and thinly, on the river bluffs.

THE SOIL AND CLIMATE.

Minnesota has, for the most part, a very fertile soil, blackened by decaying vegetation to a depth varying from one to three feet. Nine-tenths of its whole area are adapted for cultivation. Much of the State has a clayey but somewhat sandy soil, with few stones or boulders formed of the unmodified glacial drift or till. Considerable areas, principally in the northeastern half of the State, are the stratified sand and gravel of the modified drift, with a fertile black superimposed layer from one to three feet thick. In southeastern Minnesota a large district, which was not covered by the ice sheet and its glacial drift, is overspread by a deposit of modified drift, forming a very rich, loamy soil. The pulverized limestone which is a main ingredient of the drift throughout the State, excepting in the region of Lake Superior, is one of the most useful elements of the soil for the production of wheat, corn, oats and potatoes. The generally rolling surface of this State gives excellent drainage, excepting about the head waters of the Mississippi. The snow-water is thus speedily carried off in the spring, early sowing is possible, and damage by excessive rains is prevented. The rainfall is usually quite uniformly distributed through the successive seasons of spring, summer and autumn.

The snow-fall is rarely heavy, but the cold is sufficiently continuous to keep the ground covered with snow during the winter months. The extremes of temperature mark a wide range of thermometric variation, but the severity of winter is largely modified by the dry, bracing character of the air, whilst the heat of summer days is almost invariably redeemed by refreshingly cool nights. Observations extending over a term of thirty-five years record a mean temperature in spring and autumn of 45° 46', Fahrenheit; in summer of 70° 36', and in winter of 16° 6'. A careful comparison, based upon these observations, shows a mean spring and autumn temperature nearly equal to that of Chicago, two degrees and a half south, and a mean temperature throughout the year equalling that of central New York, two degrees south.

STRATIGRAPHIC GEOLOGY.

EOZOIC OR ARCHÆAN SERIES.

From the northwest side of Lake Superior a broad belt of metamorphic rocks, belonging to the Eozoic or Archæan series, extends southwest across Minnesota. On our northern boundary it reaches west to the Lake of the Woods. In the central part of the State its extreme outcrops are five miles northwest of Motley, and eastward are at the falls of Snake river, having there a width of seventy miles. The exposures of these rocks nearest to St. Paul and Minneapolis are about sixty miles distant to the northwest, in the vicinity of St. Cloud and Sauk Rapids. At this latitude they are visible in occasional or frequent outcrops for more than fifty miles, from a limit on the east at the west edge of Mille Lacs county, in northeastern Benton county, and at the quarries southeast of St. Cloud, and on the west at Sauk Center and Ashley, Stearns county. Farther west and northwest throughout Minnesota the bed-rock is universally concealed by the glacial drift. The deeply eroded valley in which the Minnesota river flows exposes these rocks at many places from the mouth of Big Stone lake to New Ulm, showing that their area in southwestern Minnesota has a breadth of one hundred miles. They are mainly granites and gneisses, rarely including masses of syenite and hornblende schist, and their prevailing strike is from northeast to northwest, at right angles with the valley. Within ten to twenty miles southwest from the Minnesota river several outcrops of granite, gneiss and schists have been found in Yellow Medicine and Redwood counties, beyond which they are covered by the drift and by thick Cretaceous deposits, and next rise to view in the Black Hills of southern Dakota.

A large area in Stearns, Benton and Sherburne counties, including the valuable quarries of St. Cloud, Haven, Sauk Rapids and Watab, consists of syenite, and exhibits no laminated or gneissic structure. It has great variety in texture as to its coarseness of grain and readiness to be quarried and wrought to any required form. Its color is mostly light gray, but upon some extensive tracts it has a red tint, similar to that of the celebrated granite of Aberdeen in Scotland. In other portions of the Eozoic district granite, gneiss and mica schist are the common rocks, sometimes associated with syenite. Their strike is usually to the northeast or east northeast. At Little Falls and Pike Rapids, and for several miles to the south, west and north, as also in northern Todd county, and along the falls of the St. Louis river above Fond du Lac, and thence northeastward, is a group of rocks quite different from the foregoing, its range of variation being from a highly cleavable clay slate, and from a mica schist, enclosing many crystals of staurolite, and sometimes garnets and iron pyrites, to a very compact, tough and massive diorite.

Comparing these rocks in Minnesota with the divisions recognized by geologists in the metamorphic rocks of Canada and elsewhere, the syenites, granites and gneisses appear to represent the Laurentian system; while the slate, staurolitic schist and diorite are probably Huronian. The great depth of the drift upon the region occupied by these crystalline rocks in Minnesota makes it impossible to draw their boundaries definitely. Westward, they probably extend to a line running a little west of south from the Lake of the Woods, to the mouth of Big Stone lake, then curving south, southeast and east to New Ulm. No exposure of the rocks underlying the drift has been found in the part of Minnesota drained by the Red river of the North, west of this line. Eastward, this boundary, separating the metamorphic area and that of the Silurian rocks of the Potsdam, lower Magnesian and Trenton periods, reaches from New Ulm north north-easterly to northern Kanabec county, and thence northeast to near Fond du Lac. Onward, along the northwestern shore of Lake Superior, the interstratification and mingling of sedimentary and eruptive rocks, the former exhibiting various degrees of metamorphism, present difficult questions respecting their age, sequence and equivalence.

PALEOZOIC SERIES.

The red sandstone of Lake Superior, quarried at Fond du Lac, and exposed at many places along the shore of the lake and thence north-eastward to Pigeon point, is considered by Prof. N. H. Winchell, as originally by Foster and Whitney, to be the equivalent of the Potsdam sandstone of New York. It is often changed to quartzyte, and is associated with metamorphic shales, slates and conglomerate, besides being in many portions cut by dikes and interbedded with immense outflows of igneous rock. This is the group called Kewanawan by Professors Chamberlin and Irving of the Wisconsin geological survey. Some of its igneous and tufaceous beds are exposed on the Kettle river at and above its junction with the St. Croix, on the Snake river for three miles below Chengwatana, and on the St. Croix river at Taylor's Falls. A red quartzyte which seems to be quite certainly the same formation with the red quartzyte, sandstone and shales of Lake Superior, outcrops in the valley of the Minnesota river at Redstone, nearly opposite New Ulm; and again in the northern part of Cottonwood county, extending into the adjoining edges of Watonwan and Brown counties, forming a massive ridge, nearly twenty-five miles long from east to west, mostly covered by glacial drift. The same quartzyte has frequent outcrops at Pipestone City and the Mound, near Luverne, in the most southwestern counties of Minnesota. The famous red pipestone quarry of the Indians is at Pipestone City, where the pipestone, or Catlinite, a very fine and durable red stone, without grit and susceptible of a fine polish, forms a layer about one foot thick, overlaid and underlaid by the very hard and coarse quartzyte.

Next in age after the preceding, is a succession of formations of sandstone and magnesian limestone, which may be called the Lower Magnesian series, shown by their fossils to be the equivalents of the Calciferous sandrock and its associated formations in the eastern states. This series of strata is exhibited in the bluffs of the St. Croix and Mississippi rivers, and reaches thence to the valley of the Minnesota river, where it has many exposures in Blue Earth county and thence northward to Shakopee. The five divisions of this group, in ascending order, are as follows: The Saint Croix sandstone, 400 to 900 feet thick; the St. Lawrence limestone, about 200 feet thick; the Jordan sandstone, 25 to 50 feet or more in thickness; the Shakopee limestone, about 100 feet thick; and the St. Peter sandstone, 75 to 125 feet or more in thickness. These beds are nearly horizontal, or dip only a few degrees.

Overlying the St. Peter sandstone, as seen in the bluffs of the Mississippi at Minneapolis, Ft. Snelling and St. Paul, is the Trenton limestone, mostly 25 to 35 feet thick. Next above this are beds of shale, about one hundred feet thick, containing thin layers of limestone, believed to belong to the Cincinnati or Hudson river group. Both these formations are plentifully fossiliferous. In the most southeastern counties of Minnesota, the Trenton limestone is overlaid by the Magnesian Galena limestone, of which a thickness of about 100 feet is seen in this State.

The only exposure of Upper Silurian rocks in Minnesota is in the north edge of Fillmore county, where a small patch of Niagara limestone is found.

Strata of Devonian limestone occupy a considerable part of Fillmore and Mower counties.

The Carboniferous series, which contains valuable coal-beds in central Iowa, apparently does not reach into Minnesota. If it enters at all into this State, it is to the west of these Upper Silurian and Devonian rocks, where the surface is deeply covered by glacial drift and shows an outcrop of rock.

MESOZOIC SERIES.

The western two-thirds of Minnesota appear to have been overspread more or less completely by Cretaceous deposits, continuous with their great area in the region drained by the upper Missouri river. There are frequent exposures of Cretaceous clays, shale and sandstone along the Minnesota river from Big Stone lake to Mankato; and at several places lignite occurs in thin seams, seldom equaling a foot in thickness. Similar Cretaceous beds are found in Mower and Stearns counties. Fragments of lignite occur frequently in the drift of all that part of Minnesota west of a line drawn from the west end of Hunter's Island, on the Canadian boundary line, southward to Minneapolis, and thence southeastwardly through Rochester to the Iowa boundary. Upon the region west of this line Cretaceous strata exist, at least, in patches, and perhaps once existed continuously.

THE DRIFT.

The next formations, overlying all the preceding and constituting the surface of the land generally throughout the state, are the glacial drift and the accompanying water-deposits of modified drift.

In the epoch when the ice-sheet that covered the north half of this continent extended to its farthest southern limit, all of Minnesota was buried under ice, averaging probably a mile or more in thickness, excepting a comparatively small district on the southeast edge of the state. This includes Houston county, most of Winona county, and portions of Fillmore and Wabasha counties. It is part of the driftless area, about 150 miles long from north to south and 100 miles wide, lying in southwestern Wisconsin and adjoining parts of Illinois, Iowa and Minnesota, which was, singularly, exempt from glaciation, while the surrounding region and a wide area farther south were covered by the ice and its glacial drift. The picturesque bluffs of rock along the Mississippi from Lake Pepin to LaCrosse and southward, often standing out isolated and alone like the ruins of turretted castles, are in this area which is uncovered by till, unmarked by striæ, and unplaned or smoothed by the ice-sheet.

In northeastern Minnesota, from Lake Superior and northern Wisconsin to the Mississippi river, the courses of striæ, or marks scratched by the slowly moving ice upon the rock beneath, and the direction in which boulders and the other materials of the drift have been carried, show that the ice moved toward the southwest. The till has a reddish color, because of the hematite, or anhydrous sesquioxide of iron, contained in the red quartzyte, sandstone, and shales of Lake Superior, which were eroded by the ice-sheet. The modified drift upon this part of the state has usually the same color. In western Minnesota the ice flowed southward from Lake Winnipeg to Big Stone lake, and thence southeast into northern Iowa, spreading a dark bluish till with many boulders of limestone. The upper part of this till, however, to a depth varying from 5 to 50 feet, has assumed a yellowish color, due to the influence of air and water upon the iron contained in the deposits, changing it from the protoxide state to hydrated sesquioxide. Most of the limestone boulders that occur in the drift throughout the western two-thirds of the State, are similar to limestone strata found in Manitoba: these are their nearest outcrops, but they may underlie the drift in portions of western and northwestern Minnesota. The boulders of granite, syenite, gneiss, and schist, which abound here, have been derived from the Laurentian highlands north of Lake Superior, and from the broad area of these rocks which reaches southwestward to the Minnesota river. Everywhere a great part of the drift has been supplied by the rocks of the region adjoining, in the direction from which the ice-current came. Boulders and pebbles of any peculiar kind of rock which can be referred to a particular source, are most abundant within the first ten or twenty miles from their parent ledges; and they diminish in numbers and average size as the distance from their source increases. While the drift is always made up largely in this manner from the formations of its vicinity, some parts of its mass, including both fine detritus and boulders, were gathered at great distances. Fragments of Laurentian rocks in the till south and west of Minnesota, appear to have been carried by the ice-sheet from 500 to 700 miles.

A very remarkable feature of our glacial deposits is their great depth. The old rocks are almost everywhere concealed upon the western two-thirds of the State; nor are they often reached by the deepest wells, which go down from 75 to 250 feet without passing through the drift. In all that part of the State the drift probably averages as deep as along the course of the Minnesota river, where a channel cut down in many places to the older rocks shows these superficial deposits to be from 100 to 200 feet thick.

Interglacial epochs, in which animals and plants lived in this region, are proved by their remains preserved, evidently where they were living, in stratified beds underlaid and overlaid by till. These are rarely found in this State, yet they are regarded as undeniable evidence that animals and plants lived here during temperate epochs, preceded and followed by an Arctic climate and ice-sheets like those now covering the interior of

Greenland and the Antartic continent. A bed of peat, several feet thick, is found between deposits of till in Mower county, beyond the terminal moraines of the last ice-sheet; showing that the ice had retreated and again advanced upon the land, before the latest glacial epoch.

THE TERMINAL MORAINE.

The most noticeable deposits of an alpine glacier are its terminal moraine, or the heaps of rock fragments and detritus which it carries forward to its termination. In Minnesota and adjoining states are found similar but much greater accumulations of drift which appear to have been amassed where the ice-sheet of the last glacial epoch had its termination. The only notable hills throughout the greater part of the state are of this origin. The material of these terminal and medial moraines heaped at the margin of the ice and along the lines where its opposing lobes and currents pushed against each other, is in Minnesota nearly everywhere till, or chiefly till with scanty deposits of modified drift. This till differs very notably from that of the more level areas at each side, in that the former has many more boulders, and a much larger intermixture of gravel and sand, than the latter.

In contour the morainic belts are very uneven, consisting usually of many billocks, mounds and ridges of rough outlines and broken slopes with enclosed hollows, which are sometimes nearly round. The height of the morainic elevations above the intervening hollows is generally from 25 to 75 or 100 feet. The only district where they are higher for any considerable part of the series is the Leaf hills, which through a distance of twenty miles rise from 100 to 350 feet above the adjoining country. Upon the Coteau des Prairies and the Coteau du Missouri, the moraines lie on areas of highland, to the altitude of which they appear to add 75 or 100 feet; rarely 150 or 200 feet.

The course of this formation of terminal moraines, marking the boundaries of the ice-sheet, and of medial and terminal moraines, marking the area of confluence of its vast lobes, during the last glacial epoch in Minnesota, is nearly as follows: Extending continuously from the Kettle moraine of Wisconsin, it enters Minnesota at the west side of St. Croix lake, is crossed twice by the Mississippi, 7 to 10 miles south of St. Paul and again between that city and Fort Snelling, and reaches thence northward between St. Paul and Minneapolis, to Mound View; thence it continues northward through Chisago, Pine, Kanabec, Mille Lacs, Benton, Stearns, Morrison, Crow Wing, and Cass counties, to the lakes at the head of the Mississippi, this part being accumulated by the ice-current that moved from the region of Lake Superior toward the southwest; from Itasca and Rice lakes it returns southward forming the Leaf hills, and thence stretches southeasterly through Douglass, Todd, Pope, Kandiyohi, Meeker, Wright and Hennepin counties, to Minnetonka lake and the western border of Minneapolis; thence it passes south through Carver, Scott, Dakota, Le Sueur, Rice, Waseca, Steele and Freeborn counties, by Albert Lea, and into Iowa to the vicinity of Des Moines, this part being pushed out at the east side of an extensive lobe of the ice-sheet whose central current went south and southeast; then on the west side of the same glacial lobe, its terminal moraines have been traced from central Iowa northward by Spirit Lake and Lake Benton to the head of the Coteau des Prairies, twenty miles west of Lake Traverse.

Much of this irregular curving tract consists of two or sometimes three well-marked morainic belts, composed of hilly and knolly drift, each a few miles in width, separated by a belt of smoother surface, from two or three to twenty-five miles wide.

RETREAT OF THE ICE-DRIFT.

At the final melting of the ice, a part of the drift which had been contained in its lower portion, was washed away by its streams and deposited as modified drift, forming layers of gravel, sand and fine silt, in the valleys along which the floods supplied by this melting descended toward the ocean. The abundant supply of sediment lifted these floods upon the surface of thick and wide plains, sloping with the valleys. After the departure of the ice, the supply of both water and sediment was so diminished that the streams could no longer overspread these flood-plains and add to their depth, but were henceforth occupied mainly in slow excavation and removal of these deposits, leaving remnants of them as plains or terraces above their present channel. Along the Mississippi the flood-plain of modified drift at Brainerd and St. Cloud has a height of about 60 feet above the river; at Clearwater and Monticello, 70 to 80 feet; at Dayton, 45 feet; and at Minneapolis, 25 to 30 feet above the river at the head of St. Anthony's Falls.

During the northward recession of the ice-sheet, free drainage from it could not take place in the Red river valley, because the descent of the land is northward. As soon as the border of the ice had retreated beyond the water-shed dividing the basin of the Minnesota from that of the Red river, a lake, fed by the glacial melting, stood at the foot of the ice-fields, and extended northward as they withdrew along the valley of the Red river to Lake Winnipeg, filling the valley and its branches to the height of the lowest point over which an outlet could be found. Until the ice barrier was melted upon the area now crossed by the Nelson river, thereby draining this glacial lake, its outlet was along the present course of the Minnesota river. The highest beach-line of this lake has been traced from

Lake Traverse to Maple Lake, 20 miles east of Crookston. In this distance of about 150 miles from south to north this beach ascends 125 feet, as compared with the present level-line. This is believed to measure the attraction of gravitation drawing the water of the lake toward the ice-sheet, which lay in great depth upon the north part of the continent. Because of its relation to the retreating ice-sheet, this lake has been named in memory of Professor Louis Agassiz, the first prominent advocate of the theory that the drift was produced by land-ice.

MINERALOGY.

Gold has been washed from the drift in noticeable quantities at various places in Wabasha, Olmsted and Fillmore counties. As an ingredient of the bedded rocks it has been sought in the chloritic slates at Vermilion lake, and west of Moose Lake Station in Carlton county, but recent assays do not show it in any appreciable amount in these formations.

Silver occurs native in the quartz veins of the slates in the northeastern part of the state, but no valuable deposits within Minnesota have yet been brought to light. Its most abundant occurrence is in the form of argentiferous galena. Some of the float pieces of copper found in the drift of the central and southern parts of the state also show small quantities of silver.

Copper has been mined to a small extent at French river, in several other places on the north shore of Lake Superior, and at Chengwatana and Taylor's Falls. At French river it occurs with prehnite, and is occasionally associated with small quantities of native silver. It is sparsely disseminated throughout much of the trap-rock of the region, but principally in one or two metalliferous beds, or belts. Small particles have been found in the mineral Thomsonite, at Good Harbor, Lake Superior. Pieces of native copper, varying in size from very small fragments to a mass weighing 78 pounds, have been occasionally found distributed through the drift in central and southern Minnesota, probably derived from the region of Lake Superior.

Graphite occurs in considerable amount at Pigeon point. It is disseminated in lumps of variable size through a metamorphic sandrock. It is also found in a vein about a foot thick a short distance above Thomson, at the head of the Nine Mile portage on the St. Louis river.

Galenite has been almost invariably found in trial shafts for silver in the Lake Superior region, associated with calcite, barite, pyrite and quartz; also in limited quantities in the Galena limestone in the northern part of the state. and in the St. Lawrence and St. Croix formations at Dresbach in Winona county.

Sphalerite, barite and *chalcopyrite* are also common in the shafts sunk for silver, and the two latter in the cupriferous rocks of the northern parts.

Pyrite occurs in nearly all mineral veins and rock formations. It is found in the Trenton limestone at Minneapolis, as little shining yellow specks, and in the Cretaceous shales and blue drift-clay of the western part of the state, it forms concretionary crystalline masses.

Marcasite is very common in southeastern parts, where it accompanies the Lower Magnesian limestone; also in lumps, partly altered to limonite, on the tops of the river bluffs.

Halite, or common salt, produces saline springs and artesian salt water in the northwestern part of the state, as for instance, in the deep well at St. Vincent.

Fluorite occurs in small quantities at Lester river on the north shore of Lake Superior, and in larger amount in some of the above mentioned silver shafts.

Cuprite exists in varying quantities wherever metallic copper is found in the rocks of the State.

Hematite is found in the vicinity of Vermilion lake and in the Mesabi range, occurring as extensive rich seams and beds in the metamorphic rocks. It also occurs as a red, ochreous deposit in many places.

Magnetite also occurs in large quantities in the same northwestern region, and at Rainy lake.

Menaccanite seems to be the principal magnetic mineral which enters into the igneous rocks of the cupriferous series in this State. Its abundance in certain regions has attracted attention to it as an iron ore. As iron-sand it gathers on the Lake Superior shore at Black beach, four miles west of Beaver Bay; and can be extracted from the gravel with a magnet in nearly all parts of the State.

Limonite frequently is found pseudomorphous after pyrite and marcasite; particularly in the changed marcasite found in the southeastern part of the state. As a bog ore it occurs in many places, and often stains the earth and the peat about lakes and marshes.

Pyroxene, labradorite, epidote and *chrysolite*, are principal constituents of the igneous rocks of the cupriferous series.

Amphibole, or hornblende, is widely disseminated in the syenites and crystalline schists of the state.

Garnet occurs abundantly, in small crystals, in the schists at Little Falls, in larger ones at Pike Rapids, and some of the metamorphic strata of the cupriferous formations at Duluth.

Biotite is common in the syenites at St. Cloud, and as a microscopic mineral in the rocks of the cupriferous series.

Muscovite is probably the mica that is mingled with the schists at Little Falls and at Thomson; and forms a constituent of most of the granites of the State. It is disseminated also through some of the sandstones, particularly the lower portions of the St. Croix sandstone at Dresbach. Along the northern boundary, at Rainy lake and at the Lake of the Woods, it has been seen in large foliæ. It forms the rock of Carlton's peak, occurs similarly at Beaver Bay, and constitutes low hills near the lake shore a few miles east of Beaver Bay. In some of these localities this mineral is nearly pure, and makes up the whole rock.

Orthoclase, andesite and *anorthite* are found in the cupriferous porphyries at Duluth and at Taylor's Falls; the first is an essential ingredient of the granites everywhere in the state. It is perhaps as often found with hornblende, forming syenite, as with mica, forming granite.

Oligoclase is found in an angitic quartz-dioryte at Watab, and in the syenitic granite at Sauk Rapids.

Staurolite is found in the mica schist at Pike Rapids and at the Lake of the Woods, associated with garnet.

Laumontite, a crumbling, flesh-colored mineral, is very abundant in the cupriferous rocks.

Chrysocolla occurs occasionally on the north shore of Lake Superior, and in the cupriferous rocks of Pine county. It is generally associated with chalcopyrite.

Prehnite is found at French river, containing native copper, and constituting, perhaps, one-tenth of the rock.

Thomsonite is found abundantly in the trap rocks on the north shore of Lake superior; and *lintonite* is found associated with it.

Natrolite is found at Beaver Bay, on the shore of Lake Superior, in seams in the labradorite rock, and is taken out in crusts about a third of an inch thick.

Stilbite is also common along the north shore of Lake Superior.

Talc is the basis of the talcose schist which forms conspicuous portions of the Huronian series at Vermilion lake and on the international boundary; but no important deposits of this mineral in its massive form, known as steatite or soapstone, have yet been discovered in Minnesota. It seems to be the chief ingredient in the greenish pipestone cut by the Indians at Pipestone Rapids and at Rainy lake.

Delessite is common as a product of decay in the trap rocks of the north shore of Lake Superior.

Apatite is known only as a minor but constant ingredient of the igneous rocks. The well-known fertility of the soils derived directly from the decomposition of these rocks seems to be due largely to the presence of this phosphate.

Gypsum is disseminated through the Cretaceous clays and shales in perfectly transparent crystals of selenite in the drift-clay, or till, of the western parts of the State.

Epsomite occurs in solution in the alkaline waters of the western part of the State. It is also occasionally noticed on the lower side of projecting shales of magnesian limestone, as a delicate white efflorescence.

Calcite, as the essential and principal ingredient of all limestones, is an abundant and very important mineral in Minnesota The only pure limestones, however, are the building-stone beds of the Trenton formations, as seen at Minneapolis and St. Paul, and the Niobrara limestone of the Cretaceous at New Ulm. Calcite also occurs in veins in the cupriferous trappean rocks. Calcareous tufa, or travertine, is frequent in Minnesota, being deposited by springs.

Dolomite is the characteristic mineral of the magnesian limestones of the State. In its crystalline pure form it is seldom seen separated from the massive rock. Sometimes as brown spar it is found lining cavities, or associated with calcite in geodic aggregations, as at St. Lawrence.

Siderite, in the condition of clay-ironstone, is found in occasional loose boulders in the drift, more or less converted to limonite. It probably has been derived from Cretaceous beds. As a pure carbonate, it is found in important quantities in the iron-bearing strata of the Mesabi range in northern Minnesota.

Malachite occurs sparingly in cupriferous rocks of the Lake Superior region. It is found also at Taylor's Falls and at Chengwatana, as coatings on the protected surfaces of seams in the rocks.

Mineral Coal occurs in Minnesota only in its inferior condition called lignite. Thin layers of this, seldom a foot thick, are found in Cretaceous strata at Redwood Falls, on Crow creek, and near Fort Ridgely, in the Minnesota valley, on the Cottonwood river west of New Ulm, and near the Sauk river in Stearns county. Fragments of lignite, varying in size up to three or nearly six inches or more in diameter, are sparingly scattered in the drift throughout all western Minnesota, so that frequently they are found in digging wells. The origin of these pieces is from Cretaceous beds like the foregoing that have been ploughed up by the ice-sheet. It is almost certain that no workable coal deposits exist in this state.

STATISTICS OF POPULATION, AGRICULTURE AND RAILWAY EXTENSION IN THE STATE OF MINNESOTA.

STATISTICS are of actual value only as the tabulated statements of carefully verified facts, obtained by patient inquiry and observation, repeated at regular intervals and extending over a long period of time, in order that successive results may be subjected to careful comparison.

These conditions being obtained, statistics, proper to the question, are rightly acceptable as evidence of the growth and progress of a country or community.

As such, the following tables are introduced. Selected from the best available sources of information,* and possessed of these essential qualifications they faithfully present, in a condensed form, the most valuable facts related to the three subjects which, taken together, serve as a good index of the present status and past development of the State, viz.: - population, agriculture and railroad extension.

POPULATION.

The primary causes which determine the increase or decrease of population within a given area are two in number: (1) the healthfulness of the climate or its reverse, and (2) the possibilities of natural production.

The first of these causes operates by effecting the relative number of births and deaths; the second by effecting the relative proportions of immigration and emigration.

Thus, a maximum of births and a minimum of deaths in a given locality are *prima facie* evidence of the healthfulness of its climate; a strong tide of immigration constantly setting in to a country, with no appreciable reflux, is sufficient proof of its agricultural wealth: whilst a reverse of these conditions is proof of the disadvantages of both.

That Minnesota is exceptionally well endowed in each of these respects will be readily appreciated by a brief study of the subjoined tables of population, etc.

---

*Report of the Commissioner of Statistics of the State of Minnesota for 1882; Joint Annual Report of the Chamber of Commerce and Board of Trade, 1882; Compendium of the U S. Tenth Census, etc., supplemented by later items under the author's direction.

THE POPULATION OF MINNESOTA FROM 1850 TO 1880.

YEAR.	TOTAL NUMBER.
1850	6,077
1860	172,023
1870	439,706
1875	597,407
1880	780,773

TABLE OF BIRTHS AND DEATHS.

YEAR.	Number of Births.	Number of Deaths.	Net Increase in Population.
1880			
1881	26,375	11,523	14,852

STATISTICS OF AGRICULTURE.

As the future of any newly settled country is dependent upon its producing power, so the foregoing facts of population may be accounted for, and the coming development of the State predicted, upon an agricultural basis.

That the advent of the people, the growth of cities, and the extension of railroads are alike conditioned upon the extent to which "the earth yields her increase," is a self-evident truth, and hence the following statistics of agriculture may be looked upon as a key to the past, present and future of Minnesota.

These tables, extracted, for the most part, from the Reports of the State Commissioner of Statistics, are computed from the latest available returns.

TOTALS OF ACREAGE AND CROPS OF 1881 AND 1882.

CROPS.	Total Acreage 1881.	Total Yield, 1881.	Average Yield per Acre.	Total Acreage, 1882.
Wheat	2,884,169	32,947,570	11.42	2,572,254
Oats	798,367	21,954,126	30.14	850,581
Corn	471,030	14,654,646	30.91	741,692
Barley	196,917	4,215,715	21.40	308,719
Rye	13,691	170,053	12.99	25,505
Buckwheat	3,564	42,847	12.02	5,116
Potatoes	41,707	3,997,187	95.84	51,351
Beans	1,703	22,294	13.09	3,868
Flaxseed	73,649	433,517		89,018
Timothy seed, bushels		46,214		
Clover seed		27,715		
Sugar cane syrup, gallons	7,396	684,686	92.49	8,105

OTHER AGRICULTURAL PRODUCTS OF 1881.

Cultivated hay, tons	227,139
Wild hay, tons	1,261,080
Butter, lbs	16,052,020
Cheese, lbs	522,452
Honey, lbs	114,162
Maple sugar, lbs., 1882	54,512
Maple syrup, gallons, 1882	12,928
Apples, bushels	158,056
Grapes, lbs	200,611
Tobacco, lbs	79,634
Wool, lbs., 1882	933,332

TOTAL YIELD OF ALL CROPS FOR THE LAST SIX YEARS.

CROPS.	1876.	1877.	1878.	1879.	1880.	1881.
Wheat, bushels	17,961,632	30,693,989	29,481,503	31,218,634	39,390,068	32,947,570
Oats, bushels	10,596,178	13,819,630	18,338,356	20,467,833	22,807,932	21,954,126
Corn, bushels	7,623,043	9,151,281	11,286,545	12,939,901	13,125,255	11,654,646
Barley, bushels	1,698,463	2,239,650	1,993,668	2,123,932	2,751,638	4,215,715
Rye, bushels	75,122	132,041	222,728	172,887	170,817	170,063
Buckwheat, bushels	66,817	79,448	37,914	33,163	29,736	42,847
Total	**37,904,285**	**56,116,019**	**60,063,044**	**67,156,450**	**78,311,446**	**73,984,957**
Beans, bushels	13,696	14,171	28,037	24,134	20,901	22,291
Potatoes, bushels	2,177,384	2,126,002	3,250,181	3,915,890	3,782,243	3,997,157
Cultivated hay, tons	135,860	131,617	155,295	194,601	175,595	227,432
Wild hay, tons	935,961	974,221	1,110,241	1,206,506	1,263,472	1,261,080
Cane syrup, gallons	102,189	140,153	329,660	446,946	602,837	681,066
Flax seed, bushels	44,213	10,838	16,982	99,378	397,190	433,517
Clover seed, bushels	5,041	8,807	7,558	18,460	8,371	27,715
Timothy seed, bushels	83,379	12,559	24,228	39,376	60,910	96,211
Tobacco, pounds	39,732	38,839	73,634	65,080	18,437	79,634
Apples, trees in bearing	153,138	156,189	258,746	260,349	255,133	267,431
Apples, bushels produced	111,538	15,736	89,862	121,261	147,888	158,058
Maple sugar, pounds		52,723	58,462	47,712	49,577	49,577
Maple syrup, gallons		16,588	10,670	12,117	13,418	13,418
Bees, number of hives	7,740	10,835	16,261	11,020	9,227	
Honey, number of pounds	101,858	213,768	253,221	208,018	221,255	114,162
Wool, pounds	640,894	705,116	790,482	918,181	923,470	1,083,775
Butter, pounds	12,318,974	13,443,195	14,873,740	15,639,060	15,663,283	16,052,020
Cheese, pounds	1,052,348	829,075	1,602,551	586,148	417,994	522,156

AVERAGE BUSHELS PER ACRE OF CROPS FOR THE LAST TWELVE YEARS.

CROPS.	1870.	1871.	1872.	1873.	1874.	1875.	1876.	1877.	1878.	1879.	1880.	1881.
Wheat	15.07	12.28	17.40	17.01	11.23	17.04	9.61	16.78	12.50	11.30	13.30	14.42
Oats	31.19	31.42	33.69	31.04	28.61	34.38	23.04	32.19	38.65	36.42	33.19	30.41
Corn	31.66	35.35	32.99	30.87	28.64	24.84	25.84	23.37	31.94	33.95	31.07	30.91
Barley	23.42	25.26	26.33	18.85	21.17	30.15	22.70	26.37	26.95	24.87	23.21	21.40
Rye	18.58	16.24	16.07	13.87	12.15	16.42	11.21	14.38	15.99	14.98	13.89	12.99
Buckwheat	16.50	15.05	13.70	10.92	9.65	12.70	7.23	11.67	9.99	9.80	10.06	12.02
Beans	13.52	13.05	12.92	12.56	7.83	9.06	7.18	1.70	12.52	11.33	13.66	13.09
Potatoes	71.91	100.40	117.89	83.31	80.94	120.76	75.75	82.00	97.12	108.26	98.87	95.84

ACREAGE OF THE PRINCIPAL CULTIVATED CROPS FOR THE LAST SIX YEARS.

CROPS.	1876.	1877.	1878.	1879.	1880.	1881.
Wheat	1,869,172	1,829,167	2,365,775	2,762,521	2,961,842	2,884,160
Oats	458,590	449,943	174,557	567,371	682,520	728,367
Corn	295,089	388,708	324,174	379,776	422,461	471,030
Barley	70,883	79,331	55,123	96,951	118,188	196,917
Rye	5,255	9,202	13,813	11,534	12,312	13,691
Buckwheat	9,240	6,095	3,706	3,380	2,955	3,564
Potatoes	32,703	40,755	35,559	37,910	38,254	41,707
Beans	1,832	3,075	2,280	2,156	1,534	1,703
Sugar cane	1,695	2,260	3,207	5,033	6,914	7,306
Cultivated hay	121,463	112,056	121,228	145,150	135,722	171,512
Flax	8,191	5,547	2,183	12,966	40,004	73,649
Miscellaneous products	13,747	18,042	27,169	18,336	24,841	19,685
Total acres	2,887,845	2 894,654	3,429,161	4,013,074	4,117,846	4,615,781
Increase over preceding year	275,480	96,809	444,510	613,910	404,772	167,935

THE CROPS OF 1881.

Total cultivated territory of the State	4,615,781	acres.
Increase in acreage over preceding year	167,935	acres.
Remaining territory possible of cultivation (about)	33,135,745	acres.

SHEEP AND WOOL FOR THE LAST TWELVE YEARS.

YEARS.	Sheep No.	Wool, lbs.
1871	116,493	355,282
1872	125,273	497,045
1873	141,749	529,659
1874	144,901	549,918
1875	143,689	578,918
1876	154,318	620,874
1877	161,797	577,067
1878	186,456	790,203
1879	206,477	948,184
1880	223 791	925,278
1881	215,453	923,170
1882	213,376	933,331

STOCK IN 1882.

Horses, number	276,690
Cattle, all ages, (including cows.)	591,794
Mules and Asses	9,664
Sheep	258,415
Hogs	279 240

COWS AND DAIRY PRODUCTS IN 1881.

Number of milch cows	221,213
Pounds of butter produced	16,052,020
Pounds of cheese produced	522,156
Number of Milch cows, 1882	231,533

SUMMARY OF DAIRY PRODUCTS FOR THE PAST ELEVEN YEARS.

YEARS.	Cows. No.	Butter, lbs.	Cheese, lbs.
1871	106,016	7,356,768	169,147
1872	135,691	8,823,630	772,030
1873	155,154	10,140,316	1,031,510
1874	169,618	10,916,912	1,080,238
1875	176,278	12,020,371	1,006,960
1876	185,149	12,318,971	1,052,318
1877	200,370	13,143,195	829,075
1878	223,413	11,873,740	1,012,551
1879	225,513	15,039,069	580,118
1880	228,055	15,693,283	417,991
1881	221,213	16,052,020	522,156

RAILWAY EXTENSION IN MINNESOTA.

Scarcely twenty-five years have elapsed since a railroad first entered the State of Minnesota, and for several years subsequent to the admission of the State to the Union (1858,)but few miles of rail were laid.

The difficulties which attended the birth and infancy of the first railway corporations have been detailed elsewhere; as also the history of the great financial embarrassment which the State has labored under in the interest of these ventures.

Freed from these misfortunes, the commonwealth may now feel a pardonable pride in the past development. the present condition and the future prospects of the great roads which intersect her boundaries and centre in her chief cities.

The nine railways which have termini in Minnesota are the owners of a grand total of 3,796.30 miles of line completed up to the present date, (August 1, 1883,) within the borders of the State.   542.37 miles of this total extent have been constructed during the past year.

These roads place her great cities in immediate connection with the whole country from St. Vincent to the Gulf, and from the Atlantic coast to Puget Sound.   They make them the inlet and the outlet for the far northwest, and as such secure their position as the natural centres of trade.

The direction, termini, and mileage of each railroad are given in the accompanying statement, to which the reader is referred.

THE RAILWAYS OF MINNESOTA.

TERMINI AND LENGTH WITHIN THE STATE TO AUGUST 1, 1883.

Chicago, Milwaukee & St. Paul Railway.

DIVISION OR FORMER NAME.	From.	To.	Miles.
River division	Bridge Junction	St. Paul	120.47
River division	St. Paul	St. Paul	8.30
River division	St. Croix Junction	Stillwater	24.90
Iowa & Minnesota division	Iowa line	Minneapolis	130.54
Iowa & Minnesota division	St. Paul Junction	St. Paul	5.61
Iowa & Minnesota division	Iowa line	Austin	11.37
Hastings & Dakota	Hastings	Ortonville	233.59
Hastings & Dakota	Minneapolis	Benton	28.90
Wabasha division	Wabasha	Zumbrota	59.00
Southern Minnesota	Grand Crossing	Dakota line	299.90
Central R. R. of Minnesota	Mankato	Wells	40.00
Chicago, Clinton, Dubuque & Minnesota	Iowa line	La Crescent	24.90
Caledonia, Miss. & Western	Caledonia Junction	Preston	57.50
Red Wing division	Northfield	Red Wing	32.00
Total			1,055.98

Chicago, St. Paul, Minneapolis & Omaha Railway.

DIVISION OR FORMER NAME.	From.	To.	Miles.
St. Paul & Sioux City	St. Paul	Iowa line	187.52
St. Paul, Stillwater & Taylor's Falls	Lake St. Croix	St. Paul	19.90
" " "	Stillwater Junction	Stillwater	3.80
" " "	Stillwater	Hudson bridge	4.39
Blue Earth branch	Lake Crystal	Elmore	44.00
Minn. & Black Hills	Heron Lake	Woodstock	44.00
Worthington & Sioux Falls	Sioux Falls Junction	Dakota line	42.53
Rock River branch	Luverne	Iowa line	10.56
Leased branch	St. Paul	Minneapolis	9.90
Total			396.60

Chicago & Northwestern Railway.

FORMER NAME OR DIVISION.	From.	To.	Miles.
Winona & St. Peter	Winona	Dakota line	288.50
Winona, Mankato & New Ulm	Mankato Junction	Mankato	3.75
Plainview	Plainview Junction	Plainview	15.01
Chatfield	Chatfield Junction	Chatfield	11.46
Rochester & North Minnesota	Rochester	Zumbrota	24.48
Minnesota Valley	Sleepy Eye	Redwood F	24.40
Chicago & Dakota	Tracy	Dakota line	46.38
Total			413.98

Minneapolis & St. Louis Railway.

FORMER NAME OR DIVISION.	From.	To.	Miles.
Main line,	Minneapolis	Iowa line	123.00
Pacific extension,	Winthrop	Morton	92.00
Total			215.00

St. Paul, Minneapolis & Manitoba Railway.

FORMER NAME OR DIVISION.	From.	To.	Miles.
Main line	St. Paul	International boundary	394.57
Main line	East Minneapolis	Moorhead	258.15
Branch	Crookston	State line	24.08
Branch	Morris	Brown's Val.	47.00
Branch	Wayzata	W. end Lake Minnetonka.	6.00
Branch	Carlisle	Elizabeth	3.70
Branch	Minneapolis	St. Cloud	82.96
Branch	St. Cloud	Hinckley	66.51
Branch	Sauk Centre	Browersville	25.75
Branch	Fergus Falls	Pelican Rapids	21.37
Branch	Shirley	St. Hilaire	21.40
Total			931.19

St. Paul & Duluth Railway.

FORMER NAME OR DIVISION.	From.	To.	Miles.
St. Paul & Duluth	St. Paul	Duluth	156.00
Stillwater & St. Paul.	White Bear	Stillwater	12.50
Knife Falls branch	North Pacific Junct	Cloquet	6.50
Taylor's Falls & Lake Superior	Wyoming	Taylor's Falls.	20.30
Minneapolis & Duluth	White Bear	Minneapolis	13.00
Total			208.30

Northern Pacific Railroad Company.

DIVISION.	From.	To.	Miles.
St. Paul	St. Paul	Brainerd	136.00
Minnesota	Duluth	Moorhead	254.50
Wisconsin	Superior	N. P. Junction	19.50
Little Falls and Dakota	Little Falls	Morris	87.75
Northern Pacific, Fergus & B. H. R. R.	Wadena	Wahpeton	77.70
Total			572.45

Minneapolis, Lyndale & Minnetonka Railway Co.

From.	To.	Miles.
Minneapolis	Excelsior	20
Total		20

Burlington, Cedar Rapids and Northern Railway.

FORMER NAME OR DIVISION.	From.	To.	Miles.
Burlington, C. R. & Northern	Iowa line	Albert Lea	12.50
Total			12.50

HISTORY

OF THE

City of Minneapolis

AND ITS SURROUNDINGS.

THE DISCOVERY OF THE FALLS OF ST. ANTHONY.

CIVILIZATION may be defined, in brief, as the power of adapting natural means to human ends, and upon the more or less perfect adaptation of these means to the highest attainable ends, rests the most appreciable advancement of the race.

To recognize and to grasp the opportunities which Nature offers—to utilize and to conserve the energy or force which she generates, is the part of genius in the process of human development.

Various and many are the occasions for its exercise; yet rarely does Nature afford any opportunity so grand or originate any power so colossal as that which is borne upon the currents of running water. In all history, the bank of a stream has been the birthplace of a colony, and from the crest of the cataract might almost be said to rise the prophecy of a city.

Long years ago far-seeing men read the future of Minneapolis in THE FALLS OF ST. ANTHONY; and to-day it is impossible to account for her growth and progress without estimating the worth of this main factor in her existence.

The water-fall is the vital element of her greatness. The great manufactories which cluster in ever increasing numbers around it, are the corner-stones of the city and the secrets of her success.

To the industries which they foster might well be applied a eulogy similar to that of Thomas Carlyle upon cotton-spinning: they are the housing of the homeless, the clothing of the naked and the feeding of the hungry in their results, —"the triumph of mind over matter in their means."

Rightly, then, may we look upon the discovery of the Falls of St. Anthony as the first unconscious beginnings of the present metropolis, and upon a brief recital of this important event as a fit introduction to her history.

Many of its details are inextricably interwoven with the preceding sketch of the State of Minnesota, but at the risk of some slight repetition, we shall again refer to the earliest records.

Louis Hennepin, the Franciscan priest, was undoubtedly the first white man who visited the great water-fall. In making the ascent of the Mississippi he does not appear to have reached this point, but in July, 1680, on returning from a sojourn with the Dakotah Indians in the neighborhood of Mille Lacs, he and his small party came in sight of the cataract.

His account of the discovery is so tinctured with the spirit of exaggeration and self-applause, which pervades all his writings, that it is very difficult to select the plain undisguised facts of the narrative.

La Salle, from whose expedition Hennepin and two followers had been detached, has recorded, at second-hand, the details of the discovery.

Placing the two reports side by side it does not seem that Hennepin was greatly impressed by the natural grandeur of the Falls; his description of them is singularly unenthusiastic, although he considered them worthy to be named after his patron-saint, St. Anthony, of Padua. His facts of measurement and of the physical features and geological appearance of the cataract are probably reliable, according, as they do, with subsequent observations; for these the reader is referred to the chapter upon local geology.

He tells us that "the curling waters," as they were named by the native tribes in the vicinity, were an object of universal worship to the Indians, who regarded them as the dwelling place of a Great Spirit, to whom, whenever they approached, they were required to bring gifts and offer prayers. This custom is reported also by later travelers.

During the period of the French dominion, the only other published account of the Falls was written by Charleville, who must certainly have borrowed his facts from Hennepin, La Salle or some unknown *voyageur*.

Nearly a century intervened between this and the next substantiated visit to the immediate neighborhood.

In 1766 Jonathan Carver, a British subject, born in Connecticut, arrived at a point just below the Falls of St. Anthony. His sketch of the scene which presented itself to him is the first attempted, and his written description is a witness to his appreciation of its natural attractions. "The country around them," he says, "is extremely beautiful. *　*　*　* On the whole, when the Falls are included, which may be seen at a distance of four miles, a more pleasing and picturesque view, I believe, cannot be found throughout the universe."

His calculations of height, etc., of the cataract, will be found with those of others, in the reports of the geological survey.

Thirty miles below the Falls he discovered a remarkable cave, which took his name, and was visited by others in later years. It has since been destroyed or concealed, and its exact location is not known.

The next recorded visitant was Lieut. Z. M. Pike, employed in the Government service, who included the Falls in his tour of observations in the year of 1805. His measurements, etc , have assisted in establishing a basis upon which the rate of recession of the Falls has been approximately determined.

Major S. H. Long, of the U. S. Engineer Corps, ascended with an exploring party, in 1817, to a point near the Falls. His superior education contributes a degree of value to his report which is not possessed by those of earlier visitors.

He describes the scene in its entirety, after discussing its minor details, as "the most interesting and magnificent ever before witnessed." In addition to observing carefully the dimensions, he gives a brief account of the geological formation of the Falls, and of the banks of the gorge.

Six years later he conducted a second expedition which was accompanied by Professor Wm. Keating, of the Pennsylvania University, who made a still more valuable report of the geology and physical features of the Falls. With this date closed what may be called the era of early exploration, and the gradual incoming of white settlers made the Falls of St. Anthony a more familiar object to American eyes. For a long period they had been looked upon as a natural wonder, but it was not until the years 1836-'7 that anyone witnessed to a recognition of the practical value of the water-power by making a land-claim upon its contiguous shores.

To Major Plympton and other officers stationed at Fort Snelling, probably belongs the credit of a partial appreciation of its vast importance in the establishment of a future city.

They failed, however, to make good their claim, being dispossessed thereof by Franklin Steele, a pioneer settler, who had almost simultaneously realized the available resources of the Falls, and asserted the validity of his claim upon the ground that his predecessors held military office, and had settled prior to completion of the treaty with the Indians ceding the land.

From this point, the history of the utilization and improvement of the Falls, which have secured to the city and the State the possession of the most remarkable water-power in the country, becomes the history of Minneapolis, and naturally merges itself therein.

A description of the geological features of the Falls, of their recession, and threatened destruction, and of the means adopted for their preservation, is given in subsequent pages.

Human skill in adapting this miracle of Nature to its own ends, has perpetuated and enhanced its usefulness, whilst in so doing it has effectually destroyed much of its former beauty.

THE PHYSICAL FEATURES, GEOLOGY, ETC., OF THE CITY OF MINNEAPOLIS AND ITS IMMEDIATE NEIGHBORHOOD.

THE city of Minneapolis is situated upon both sides of the Mississippi river at the Falls of Saint Anthony, in the east part of Hennepin county. The area included within the city limits reaches seven and one-half miles from north to south and about $6\frac{1}{4}$ miles from east to west, embracing approximately 33 square miles.

This area contains, in its southwest part, a beautiful series of lakes, namely: Cedar Lake, the Lake of the Isles, Lake Calhoun, and Lake Harriet, each about a mile in length. Bassett's creek is the principal affluent to the Mississippi from the west within the city limits, and three smaller streams fall into the river from the east.

The latitude and longitude of the smaller cupola of the main building of the University of Minnesota, in the east part of Minneapolis, as determined by the United States Lake Survey, are as follows: latitude north, 44° 58' 39''.22; longitude west from Greenwich, 93° 14' 08 '.60. It is therefore about one and a half miles south of the parallel of 45°.

References to the geology of Minneapolis and its vicinity have been made in the preceding pages, describing the physical features and geological structure of the State. The rocky strata forming the bluffs of the Mississippi below the Falls in this city, are the white, friable, unfossiliferous St. Peter sandstone at the base, and the bluish, hard, compact, fossiliferous Trenton limestone above. The latter, projecting as a shelf of rock over the easily eroded sandstone, forms the brink of the Falls of St. Anthony, of the Fawn's Leap, Silver Cascade, the Bridal Veil, and Minnehaha Falls.

The cap of limestone over the sandstone in the bed of the Mississippi river extends but a short distance along the present position of the Falls of St. Anthony; and its rapid destruction prior to the institution of measures, some years since, for its protection, threatened to convert the Falls into a foaming rapid, thus destroying, or greatly damaging, one of the most important water-powers of the world. The water, percolating through the soft sandstone caused its rapid erosion, thus undermining the foundations of the limestone, and causing the constant precipitation of the rock by its own unsupported weight. A number of streams, some of considerable size, were found thus passing through the sandstone, having entered it from the river at points above the limit of the limestone. Being under considerable hydrostatic pressure, their power of erosion was greater than ordinary surface streams of the same size.

THE PRESERVATION OF THE WATER-POWER.

The owners of the water-power had, prior to 1870, attempted its preservation by the construction of dams and canals, but it was not until that year that serious alarm was created by the constantly-noted recession of the Falls. The aid of the general Government was solicited and arrangements made to apron the Falls with heavy timber. But not long after, a new cause of danger appeared. The river breaking into a tunnel which had been constructed below the water-power for manufacturing purposes rapidly wore away the soft sandstone and further imperilled the limestone upon which depended the integrity of the Falls. The Government at Washington gave prompt and efficient aid which, together with the efforts and contributions of private citizens, and the engineering skill of Colonel Farquhar of the U. S. engineers, resulted in the permanent salvation of the water-power. In 1874-'6 an immense dyke of concrete, or beton, was erected across the river beneath the limestone ledge, effectually preventing the water from penetrating and eroding the sandstone formation beneath. This dyke has a thickness of four feet, a height of thirty-nine feet, and a length of one thousand eight hundred and seventy-five feet. The years which have elapsed since its completion have sufficiently demonstrated its power to accomplish the object for which it was built, and the consequent preservation of the Falls may be regarded as a triumph of science over the rude forces of nature. It is estimated that $924.000 have been expended upon the task, of which amount $324,000 were obtained, by subscriptions, from the citizens of Minneapolis, and $600,000 from the United States Treasury.

THE TRENTON LIMESTONE.

The section of the Trenton limestone at Minneapolis, in descending order, is as follows:—

1. Dolomitic sandstone, with much argillaceous matter, crystalline, close grained, rough and hard, but splitting lenticularly under the weather; of a blue color within,

fading to a drab under exposure, and on the immediate surface to a dirty buff. It contains abundant specimens of *Orthis tricenaria* aud *Strophomena Minnesotensis*, as well as occasionally *Murchisonia*, *Leperditia* and *Edmondia*. The fossils, however, are apt to be in the form of casts and impressions. Thickness, about eight feet.

2 Similar to the last but gradually becoming more impure with shale, the fossils being gathered more into layers, making mere calcareous belts. Thickness, two feet.

3. Green shale, calcareous, weathering blue, with but few fossils. Thickness, four feet eight inches.

4. The last passes gradually into a calcareous shale resembling the well known building rock of this place, in which there are still few distinguishable fossils. This stone is sometimes used, like No. 1 above, for rough walls, or in protected positions. It is markedly set off from the rock below by a projecting shoulder formed by the upper portion of No. 5. Thickness, two feet four inches.

5. Blue building-stone layers, used extensively at Minneapolis and Saint Paul. This stone is rather too argillaceous for reliable building material, yet it is extensively used. The shale is intimately disseminated through the calcareous layers without showing regular lamination, yet it causes a mottled, or blotched color over the surfaces when cut or broken. The darker spots are shaly; the lighter ones, which constitute the most of the rock, are more purely calcareous. The color of the whole is bluish gray, which gives it the appearance of strength and durability in a structure. The fossil remains in this layer are apt to be so comminuted as to be wholly indistinguishable, yet sometimes large pieces of *Endoceras Magnirentrum*, H , are found in the layers. Rarely also on separating the layers in quarrying, a rock surface is disclosed that is eminently fossiliferous with forms of *Rhynchonella, Orthis*, and other genera of brachiopods and incrusting corals. This is the principal and most constant member of the Lower Trenton. Thickness, thirteen feet.

6. Dolomitic limestone, somewhat vesicular, of a dirty drab color, less affected by shaly interlaminations than the last, in heavy beds that furnish a good building material. This stone is used indiscriminately with the last in all places, but is evidently a more valuable one. Thickness, two feet.

7. Blue shale, partly conchoidally under the weather, lying on the St. Peter sandstone. Thickness, three feet. Total, thirty-five feet.

The dolomitic layers are more durable than the regular building-stone. The upper dolomitic layers do not appear in the quarries near the Falls, but they are seen in the quarries near the University, and in those on the west side of the river at some distance below the Falls. The dip of the formation, and the erosions of the past, have destroyed them at and above the Falls of St. Anthony. The older portion of the State University contains a large amount of this stone, and its greater durability than that of the regular building-stone can there be seen. The lower dolomitic stone is found in all the quarries.

Above the Falls of St. Anthony the line of the edge of the limerock produces a terraced ascent facing the river, about half a mile from it, which can be traced on the west side of the river some three miles northward to Shingle creek, where it bears westwardly away from the river along the south side of the creek and becomes lost beneath the drift. On the east side, at about the same distance from the river, it runs northwardly and northeastwardly toward the junction of the railroads; and about three miles further north it is exposed and worked in one or two quarries situated on the Anoka county line, northwest of Sandy lake, near the railroad. It is evident from its condition and color at this point, and all along the terrace-like ascent formed on either side of the river above the Falls, that it has been subjected to the action of the weather through a long period of time. Indeed it is, with difficulty, recognizable as the same rock that forms the Falls of St. Anthony, without a knowledge of its stratigraphical continuity.

There is a gentle dip in the layers of the Trenton limestone at Minneapolis toward the southeast. At the lower bridge it is hardly preceptible; at the Falls it is about an inch in one hundred feet; northwestwardly it soon increases to three or four inches in a hundred feet, and at Central avenue, on the east side of the river, it is about five feet in a hundred. This dip causes the rock to rise toward the northwest from under the river and into the river banks, finally running, so already stated, half a mile or more from the river and about fifty feet above it. The dip at Central avenue does not continue the same, but decreases northwardly.

The underlying St. Peter sandstone is exposed above the Falls, on the east side of the river near the upper bridge, and on the west side at the mill-pond at Shingle creek, one mile north of the limits of the city.

Overlying the Trenton limestone, in the east part of Minneapolis, are beds of shale of greenish color, probably referable to the Hudson River formation. They are about twenty feet in thickness, but being rather soft and easily covered up, they are hidden by the overlaying drift at nearly all points along the river bluffs. Within these shales are often thin lenticular layers of very fossiliferous crystalline limestone, the upper and lower surfaces of which are literally covered with fossils in a fine state of preservation, but firmly bound to the limestone layers. There are also fossils distributed through the shales themselves, which, on weathering, wash out in perfect preservation.

THE GLACIAL DRIFT.

The glacial drift lies directly upon the Trenton limestone in the central and northwest parts of Minneapolis, and on the green shales further east. The knolls and hills of the terminal moraines of the last glacial epoch are seen at the east and west borders of the city. The eastern belt, one to two miles or more in width, composed of red till and modified drift, was accumulated by ice that advanced from Lake Superior and northern Wisconsin, moving southward. The rolling and hilly drift on the west, composed of dark bluish or gray till, weathered in its upper portion to a yellowish color, occupying a width of many miles and enclosing Minnetonka lake, forming its varied outlines of projecting points and islands, was brought from the northwest by ice that moved from Lake Winnipeg and the Red river valley toward the south and southwest.

In the earlier glacial epoch when the ice-sheets covered its greatest area, this region was deeply covered by ice, and that time may be the date of the striæ which are found on the surface of the Trenton limestone in this city, bearing S. 5° E. on Nicollet island, S. 22° E. on Hennepin island, and S. 12° E. at the quarry opposite the University.

During the epoch when the ice-sheet last overspread this region, its currents from the northeast and northwest were confluent and pushed against each other upon an area reaching from northern Dakota county to Minneapolis, and continuing northward and northwestward to the Leaf hills. In this city and westward to Minnetonka lake, and upon a large area on the north, the dark bluish or gray till, weathered on the surface to a yellowish color, containing boulders and pebbles of limestone and of Cretaceous shale and other material brought from the northwest, overlies the red till and rock-fragments from Lake Superior. This shows that, before the ice disappeared from this district, its current from the northwest became stronger and extended farther eastward than in the former part of this glacial epoch, pushing back the opposing ice-current which came from the northeast.

Minneapolis is mostly built on the plain of modified drift or beds of gravel, sand and clay, which were deposited by the floods that were poured along the valley of the Mississippi river from the retreating ice-fields at the final melting. This modified drift occupies a width varying from one and a half to four miles on the west side of the Mississippi from Minneapolis to Fort Snelling. It is part of the ancient glacial flood-plain of this river, having a thickness in Minneapolis of 10 to 30 or 40 feet. The till upon which it lies usually has a similar thickness between this modified drift and the bed-rock. The till, or unmodified glacial drift, forms the surface at many places near the river where the modified drift has been eroded, or where it rises above the old flood-plain; and outside the limits of this plain it rises in morainic hills. The red till from Lake Superior is found on Central avenue and generally in the north and west parts of the city, but farther west it is covered by the bluish or gray till.

THE RECESSION OF THE FALLS OF ST. ANTHONY.

The intimate connection between the history of the drift and the recession of the Falls of St. Anthony affords a datum from which Professor N. H. Winchell has computed the date of the last glacial epoch. The gorge formed by the recession of the Falls extends, with pretty nearly the same width and outward character, to Fort Snelling, a distance of about eight miles, where the river enters a gorge of a very different kind. This is an older river valley, —one which probably witnessed, at some more remote period, the recession of similar falls past the site of the Fort and up the valley of the Minnesota river toward Shakopee. The Minnesota occupies the main valley, the external character of which resembles that of the Mississippi valley below Fort Snelling,—the Mississippi river above the union of the two rivers being only a subordinate tributary. The Minnesota, although smaller at the present time than the Mississippi, shows evidence of greater age, and of having flowed in greater volume during some period of its history.

The principal points of difference between the Mississippi valley above Fort Snelling and the greater valley which it enters in at that place are as follows: The gorge of the Mississippi above the Fort is about a quarter of a mile wide; below the Fort it is a mile wide, the same width continuing up the Minnesota valley. The walls of the gorge of the Mississippi above the Fort have the appearance of having been freshly broken, the rock lying in uncovered fragments in a talus at the base; the older valley, on the other hand, is flanked by bluffs that are rounded off, the fragments being hidden by a loam or by drift gravel, so that they are turfed over or even wooded. The limestone in the bluffs above the Fort is visible without interruption from the Fort to the Falls of St. Anthony; in the older valley below the Fort it is only interruptedly exposed, and is cut out and broken down by other small tributary streams, and above the Fort the outcrop of the Trenton limestone is soon lost sight of under a thick covering of drift.

There is a perpendicular section of the drift running along the top of the limestone in the Mississippi valley above the Fort, as if the drift had fallen when the rock that supported it gave way. The drift section abuts immediately upon the river, and forms a part of the high bluffs that enclose it; in the old valley which the Mississippi joins, the drift has been deposited *within the rock bluffs* and hides them, and there is no natural perpendicular section of drift materials running along the tops of the bluffs. The direction of the Mississippi above the Fort is toward the southeast; but after entering the old valley it turns at a right angle and runs northward, that being also the direction of the Minnesota above the Fort.

There is also another point in connection with the description of this gorge to which it is necessary to direct attention. The foregoing facts are alone sufficient to suggest to the reflective observer some difference in the age of these two portions of the great valley. When, however, it is found that above the Falls of St. Anthony, but within the corporate limits of Minneapolis, the rock bluffs which so closely confine the river below the

Falls within the width of a quarter of a mile are suddenly diverted from the river, running inland about a mile apart, covered with glacial and modified drift like the bluffs below the Fort, it becomes evident that here the Mississippi is running in an ancient channel, and for some reason the course of that great river has been changed, the narrow gorge that extends between the Falls and Fort Snelling being, of course, the new cut.

AN ANCIENT RIVER-CHANNEL.

On tracing out the range of the rock-bluff on the west side of the Mississippi above the Falls, hidden as that bluff is by loam and drift, it is found to fall rapidly away from the river near the railroad bridge, turning southward across the city, ascending the south side of Bassett's creek, which joins the river some distance farther up, and finally passing out of sight in a southwesterly direction under a thick accumulation of drift.

Going now across Bassett's creek, and taking the outcrop of the limestone, we pass over a wide valley filled with alluvium or brick clay—much too large a valley to have been formed by the sluggish creek that now runs through it. We find that the limestone, which along the river has a trend a little west of south, on reaching the valley of the creek swings more westwardly, parallel with the outcrop of the rock on the south side of the creek, and thus encloses a valley, even a gorge, cut in the limestone and sandstone, much wider than the gorge now being cut by the recession of the Falls, but in width corresponding with that between the rock-bluffs above the mouth of Bassett's creek and comparable to that below Fort Snelling.

Here, then, we have an old drift-filled valley, evidently formed at some more remote period than the present, which once held the Mississippi as it ran between rock-bound bluffs towards the Minnesota, and reached that great valley at some point between Fort Snelling and Shakopee. Bassett's creek, in making its way to the Mississippi, falls into the depression caused by the old valley in question, and follows it till it reaches the present river-channel. This ancient drift-filled valley is over one hundred feet deep. This has been ascertained by the borings made for deep wells, and the materials which fill it up are found to be till and fine stratified clay, from below which rises artesian water.

Such ancient buried river-channels are not uncommon. A number have been described in various parts of the United States. It is not common, however, that circumstances should so have combined as to produce, by the change of course of a river and the burial of its old valley, a retreating waterfall, which, by its uniform rate of recession, fixes the date of such change. Niagara river has thus been changed, but its rate of recession has not been uniform, owing to changes in the nature of the rock undergoing the process of erosion, and to a dip in all the formations toward the south, which, of course, gradually diminishes the height of the Falls. There seems also to be no recognized datum-point by which to establish a rate of recession.

THE RATE OF RECESSION.

It is not possible to calculate the time required for the recession of the Falls of St. Anthony from Fort Snelling by relying on the known recession since the settlement of the region, though they have gone back about five hundred feet. This extraordinary rate has been caused by artificial means, chiefly by the construction of saw-mills and dams, directing thereby the current or concentrating it on certain points, and by the passing of logs over the Falls. We must have recourse to historical data. Fortunately we have records of the appearance of the Falls at different times, by which we can fix their position.

They were discovered by Louis Hennepin, in July, 1680, who described the cataract as a "fall fifty or sixty feet in height, and having an island of rock in the form of a pyramid in the middle of the *chute*."

Jonathan Carver, who visited the Falls of St. Anthony in 1766, thus describes them: "This amazing body of waters, which are about 250 yards over, form a most pleasing cataract; they fall perpendicularly about 30 feet, and the rapids below, in the space of 300 yards more, render the descent considerable greater. * * * In the middle of the Falls stands a small island, about 40 feet broad and somewhat longer, on which grow a few hemlock and spruce trees; and about halfway between this island and the eastern shore is a rock lying at the very edge of the Falls in an oblique position, that appeared to be 5 or 6 feet broad, and 30 or 40 long. * * * At a little distance below the Falls stands a small island of about an acre and a half."

Lieut. Z. N. Pike visited the Falls, in the service of the United States Government, in September, 1805. His journal reads as follows: "On an actual survey, I find the portage to be 260 poles; but when the river is not very low, boats ascending may put in 31 poles below, at a large cedar tree, which would reduce it to 229 poles. The hill on which the portage is made is 69 feet ascent, with an elevation at the point of debarkation of 45°. The fall of the water between the points of debarkation and reloading is 58 feet; the perpendicular fall of the chute is $16\frac{1}{2}$ feet; the width of the river above the chute is 627 yards, below 209."

Major Stephen H. Long visited the Falls of St. Anthony in a six-oared boat in 1817. The following is his account: "The perpendicular face of the water at the cataract, as stated by Pike, in his journal, is sixteen and a

4

half feet, which I found to be true by actual measurement. To this height, however, four or five feet may be added for the rapid descent which immediately succeeds the perpendicular fall within a few yards below. Immediately at the cataract the river is divided into two parts by an island, which extends considerably above and below the cataract, and is about 500 yards long. The channel on the right side of the island is about three times the width of that on the left. The quantity of water passing through them is not, however, in the same proportion, as about one-third part of the whole passes through the left channel. In the broadest channel, just below the cataract, is a small island also, about fifty yards in length and thirty in breadth; both of these islands contain the same kind of rocky formation as the banks of the river, and are nearly as high. Besides these there are, immediately at the foot of the cataract, two islands of very inconsiderable size, situated in the right channel also. The rapids commence several hundred yards above the cataract, and continue about eight miles below. The fall of the water, beginning at the head of the rapids, and extending two hundred and sixty rods down the river to where the portage-road commences, below the cataract, is according to Pike, fifty-eight feet. If this estimate be true, the whole fall from the head to the foot of the rapids is not probably much less than one hundred feet."

In 1823 Major Long again visited the Falls of St. Anthony on his way up the Minnesota river. Professor Keating, of the University of Pennsylvania, who accompanied him as geologist and naturalist, thus describes the Falls: "An island, stretched in the river both above and below the fall, separates it into two unequal parts, the eastern being two hundred and thirty yards wide, and the western three hundred and ten. * * * * Concerning the height of the fall and breadth of the river at this place, much incorrect information has been published. Hennepin, who was the first European who visited it, states it to be fifty or sixty feet high. * * * * This height is by Carver reduced to about thirty feet; his strictures upon Hennepin, whom he taxes with exaggeration, might with great propriety be retorted upon himself; and we feel strongly inclined to say of him, as he said of his predecessor. 'The good father, I fear, too often had no other foundation for his accounts than report, or at least a slight inspection.' * * * * Mr. Calhoun measured it while we were there with a rough water-level, and made it about fifteen feet."

SUMMARY OF HISTORICAL DATA.

The above statements may be summarized, and the following data arrived at:—

HENNEPIN, 1680.—Pyramidal rocky island dividing the fall near the middle. Height of the fall, fifty or sixty feet.

CARVER. 1766.—Width of river 250 yards; height of the fall, 30 feet; a small island in the middle of the fall 40 feet broad and "somewhat longer," and another of an acre and a half a little below the falls; an island also above the Falls, shown by the sketch engraved in his book; an oblique rock in the brink of the Falls, halfway between the island and the east shore, "about five or six feet broad and thirty or forty long."

PIKE, 1805. -The waterfall, 16½ feet; width of the river above the falls, 627 yards, below 209; portage, 260 poles.

LONG, 1817.—An island, five hundred yards long, separated the cataract into two parts, extending also above and below the Falls; the fall on the west side is three times as wide as that on the east; but one-third part of the water descends the east channel. A small island, 50 yards by 30, just below the cataract in the west channel. The islands are rocky, with the same formation as the banks, "and nearly as high;" two others, of fallen fragments and of small size, near the foot of the cataract in the west channel.

KEATING, 1823.—An island in the river both above and below the cataract, separating it into two unequal parts, the eastern 230 yards, and the western 310 yards wide, the island itself being 100 yards wide; below the fall the river contracts to about 200 yards.

By combining and adjusting these statements with each other, a continued record is found of the appearance of the Falls since their discovery, and by the present existence of islands in the channel and in the cataract the position of the Falls at certain dates may be satisfactorily established. When they were discovered by Hennepin they were divided by Spirit island, and were much higher than now, owing probably to the contraction of the gorge below the Falls. The gorge across Spirit island has a width of 1350 feet, determined by a system of triangulation by Mr. M. D. Rhame; while the width of the gorge, including Hennepin island, is 1700 feet at the point where the Falls were in 1856. Below Spirit island the gorge becomes still narrow. When Carver saw the Falls in 1766, they appear to have been just leaving Spirit island and entering on Hennepin island. Lieutenant Pike makes no mention of any island in the Falls in 1805, though he gives a description of the Falls themselves. When he arrived Spirit island must have been wholly below the Falls, and Hennepin island must have come farther into them, as described by Major Long in 1817. That island then divided them unequally, the main channel being on the west side of the island. In 1823 Keating reports the same general description. It is tolerably well known where the Falls were in 1856. The Falls in the channel have not receded perceptibly since that date, while those in the west channel have gone back about 500 feet, as already stated.

The most careful measurement ever made of the river between Fort Snelling and the Falls of St. Anthony was conducted by Gen. G. K. Warren. His maps make the distance almost exactly eight miles. A series of triangulations has been made with a view of ascertaining as nearly as possible the amounts of recession since Hennepin's and Carver's visits. The interval between Carver's time and 1856 is regarded as the most reliable datum, because the statements of Hennepin do not determine at what point in Spirit island he saw the crest of the Falls. Still, for the purpose of comparison, a point has been assumed on Spirit island, and from it measurements have been made, it being presumed that Hennepin saw the Falls when they were near the middle of this island. The survey makes the recession between the discovery of the Falls and Carver's visit 300 feet; between Carver and 1856, 606 feet; and the whole recession since Hennepin in 1680, 906 feet. This gives us three rates of recession, as follows: (1), Between Hennepin and Carver, 3.49 feet per year; (2), between Carver and 1856, 6.73 feet per year; and (3), between Hennepin and 1856, 5.15 feet per year. The times required for the recession from Fort Snelling would be respectively: (1), 12,103 years; (2), 6,276 years; and (3), 8,202 years. The average of these is 8,859.

PRE-HISTORIC RECESSION.

Now, this only expresses the time involved in the recession from Fort Snelling, which is several miles above St. Paul. There must have been a prior time when the Falls were at St. Paul, and even below that point, inasmuch as the same conjunction of circumstances and the same formation extends several miles below that city. It is not probable, however, that any data will be discovered for computing that period of recession; it must have been during the preglacial times and nearly all the traces of that history have been obliterated by the ice of the glacial period. That recession must have continued past Fort Snelling, along the old valley, and toward Shakopee; and from some point in the Minnesota valley the falls of the Mississippi river may have receded, and probably did, through the intervening portion of Hennepin county, by Lakes Harriet and Calhoun, to the wide valley occupied by Bassett's creek, eroding this and the wide Mississippi valley above Bassett's creek. This preglacial channel is in the area where the opposing ice-currents of the last glacial epoch were confluent; and it has been choked up and deeply covered by the glacial and modified drift. The river thus crowded out of its old valley took a new course farther east; and at the point where it re-entered its abandoned channel or valley, it gave origin to the postglacial falls of St. Anthony by plunging over the limestone in which the old channel had been excavated.

The gorge since formed, eight miles in length, reaching from Fort Snelling to the present place of the Falls, is postglacial; and the time occupied in its excavation extending from the date when the ice-sheet disappeared till now, is estimated, by the historical data here stated, to be about 8,000 years.

The Falls of Minnehaha, 50 feet high, have cut a gorge about a half mile long, joining that of the Mississippi above Fort Snelling and about six miles from Minneapolis.

THE SETTLEMENT AND GROWTH OF THE CITY OF MINNEAPOLIS.

THE germ of a great city lies in its natural position, which must needs be endowed with one or more primary qualities essential to its development : and in proportion as these qualities are possessed and blended with each other will its future greatness be assured.

Its situation must be one to which a large and productive area of country is necessarily tributary; or it must stand as a natural centre of trade and an established centre of population ; or it must serve as an inlet for immigration and an outlet for the shipment and distribution of crops ; or it must contain within its own probable limits means possible of adaptation to manufacture.

That Minneapolis has her strongest *raison d'etre* in her exceptionally perfect possession of this last great qualification for greatness, we have already shown, but that she has reached a point of development at which she becomes practically independent of any *one* element of success, is due to the fact that she combines, in an extraordinary manner, each and all of these alternative essentials.

The city commands a superb agricultural region, only, as yet, imperfectly utilized, which is simply imperial in extent; as the terminus of railways radiating to all points of the compass, she is fast becoming a general commercial depot for the whole of this vast area; as the main gateway to "the new Northwest," the tides of immigration set strongly towards her, whilst an immense supply of staples passes daily outward to the markets of the world : and, finally, upon the banks of her great water-power, not one-fifth of which is yet employed, stands a growing group of factories preparing for human consumption the varied products of the soil.

So recent and so almost phenomenally rapid has been the growth of the city of Minneapolis that it is a matter of especial interest to trace out in brief retrospect, the path of her progress from its earliest beginnings to the near present. Seldom can a local history, pregnant with such great results, be written in so condensed a form.

A DUAL ORIGIN. The present city of Minneapolis embraces not only the corporation originally organized under that name, but also the former city of St. Anthony. The early years of the history of each must therefore be sketched separately up to the time of their union. In point of age, St. Anthony has the priority, while in size she was quickly outstripped by her younger and more fortunate sister.

EARLY SETTLEMENT OF ST. ANTHONY. As already recorded in the history of the Falls, the first persons to select and stake out claims upon the East Side of the river were Major Plympton and other officers of Fort Snelling. Their military position, however, together with their too early anticipation of the cession of the land by the Indians, combined to prejudice the legality of their occupation. Franklin Steele entered, in 1837, upon the coveted claim, which included the Falls upon that side of the river, and built a log cabin upon it. He was soon followed by others, and experienced some difficulty in holding his possessions.

In 1845, Pierre Bottineau, who was held in great repute as a guide by the early settlers, also established himself upon the present site of St. Anthony, and purchased several very valuable claims. Some fifty persons were then resident within the after limits of the city. Two years later Wm. A. Cheever settled near the site of the State University, and conducted negotiations between Franklin Steele and certain Eastern capitalists, which resulted in the purchase by the latter of the East side waterpower at a cost of $12,000. The erection of saw-mills was at once started, and the first to be completed beyond the limits of the military reservation, was running in the year following.

In 1848 the first ferry was constructed across the Mississippi, at St. Anthony, not far from the present Suspension Bridge.

In 1849 St. Anthony held some three hundred people; the first school was started in a little cabin, some stores built, and a post-office established. A library association was also founded, and other social refinements witnessed to the improving character of the settlers and the growth of the new city.

In the next two years, churches appeared, the first survey of the town was completed, and the pioneer newspaper, entitled "The St. Anthony Express," published.

In 1854 and 1855 the first suspension bridge was built, and was largely instrumental in the spread of business from the East side, where it had been altogether concentrated, to the West.

During the latter year the city of St. Anthony was incorporated by act of the Legislature, and its first council chosen.

In 1856 the erection of the University of Minnesota was begun.

The control of the water-power, which had hitherto remained in individual hands, was vested, at this time, in two companies, the one known as "The St. Anthony Water-Power Company," and the other as "The Minneapolis Water-Power Company." The erection of mills, which had been constantly on the increase, was stimulated by the transfer.

St. Anthony now boasted 105 business places, several churches and hotels, and a large and growing number of residences, but the town suffered in common with the whole country, in the general financial paralysis of 1857.

The year 1860 saw the organization of a full municipal government, and that of 1862 the completion of the first railroad between St. Anthony and St. Paul.

THE UNION OF THE SISTER CITIES. From this time until her union with the city of Minneapolis, the growth of St. Anthony was steady and substantial. As the former city gradually took the lead, business was, in some measure, carried across the river, and the destruction, by fire and other means, of several mills, put an end, for some years, to the milling interests upon the East side where they had been first established. In 1872, despite the reluctance of many of her citizens, a union of the two corporations was effected by act of Legislature, and St. Anthony lost her separate identity.

FIRST SETTLEMENT IN MINNEAPOLIS. The land upon which the city of Minneapolis now stands, was originally included, for the most part, within the limits of the Government reservation attached to Fort Snelling, and this fact long proved a hindrance to its settlement, and an embarrassment to those who had the temerity, nevertheless, to establish themselves upon it. The first settlers were the Swiss, who were driven, by hardship, from the impoverished Selkirk Colony, and arrived at the Fort in the year 1826. Despite of the discouragements they met with from the officers, they dwelt upon the reservation for nearly ten years, when, by order of the Government, they were forcibly removed, and obliged to seek new homes in St. Paul, or in parts of Wisconsin.

They were a farming community, and so distinctly rural in their tendencies, that they cannot be regarded as bearing any part in the formation of the coming city.

PIONEER SETTLERS. The actual pioneer of Minneapolis was Col. J. H. Stevens, who, with ten others, arrived in April, 1849, and settled at St. Anthony. He was determined, however, to establish himself upon the West side of the Mississippi, and by special permission of the Government, he was allowed to occupy a claim upon the reservation, where he built a log house and wintered in it with his family. One of his daughters, since deceased, was the first white child born within the limits of Minneapolis.

In the same year he was followed by C. A. Tuttle and others, who built houses in the immediate neighborhood, and by the end of 1850 a small colony of cabins marked the foundations of the future metropolis.

Hon. Robert Smith leased the old Government house and mill, built upon the reservation in 1821, and occupied a claim by a like special permission as Col. Stevens obtained, but the majority of these early settlers established themselves upon the reservation in the hope that they would finally be permitted to "prove up" their claims. They were duly warned to the contrary, but persisted in their occupation, and formed a land association for their mutual protection and benefit. When, in 1854, the authorities directed the public sale of these lands, they despatched to Washington a delegation of citizens, who were successful in obtaining a "stay of proceedings," and finally in securing the passage through Congress of an act providing for the reduction of the reservation, and granting to the settlers the privilege of pre-empting the lands. In the spring of 1855 they were allowed to "prove up" their claims and secure their titles.

The reduction of the reservation caused a great increase of the population, and opened the way for the speedy upgrowth of the new city.

During the year 1854 more than a hundred houses and nine stores were built, and the place received its name.

In 1855 a number of other stores were put up, and four churches were established.

The financial depression of 1857 temporarily crippled the growth of the town, and caused much property to change hands at a heavy loss.

Already the population had reached 2,000, 42 business houses had started, a court house and a costly school building were in process of erection, a Board of Trade was established, two saw mills were running on the West side of the river, and four physicians and ten lawyers were practicing in their respective professions. In the year 1858 Minneapolis was incorporated, under a town government, but so burdensome were the expenses attending the new venture, and the corporation was so heavily taxed, that the citizens requested the Legislature to repeal the charter in

1862, and the city was re-organized under township management. The first flouring mill on the West side of the river was completed in 1859, and another in 1860.

Three additional mills followed in 1863, 1866 and 1867. It was not until 1867 that an act was again passed, providing for the reincorporation of the city. During the intervening years the growth of Minneapolis was gradual, and from this period to the present stage of development will be best observed by a brief glance at the progress of her business and public interests in detail.

The union of the two cities under public charter, in the year 1872, has been already noted; an alliance which promoted the resulting corporation of Minneapolis to the rank of large cities.

The Minneapolis of 1883 placed in comparison with the city of ten years since, by means of the estimates and tables which fill the following pages, witnessed to a growth equalled only by that of Chicago and beyond that of any other city in the Union.

THE POPULATION OF MINNEAPOLIS.

WITH the single exception of Chicago, no other American city has ever had the remarkably rapid growth in population, which has, so far, signalized the history of Minneapolis.

Whatever future may be in store for the city, her *past* is, even by Chicago, unexcelled.

Twenty-eight years of existence had done no more for the latter than they have accomplished for her northern neighbor; and there is no discernible reason why the present rate of increase should not persist indefinitely, until Minneapolis takes rank among the largest cities in America.

All the conditions which favor growth are combined in a more than ordinary degree; nature and art seem to vie with each other in aid of human industry; the capacity of the place for development is almost unlimited, and the surrounding country, rich in but partially utilized agricultural facilities, is a continually enlarging market for supplies.

The city has gained in the year past an impetus which must carry it onward by its own intrinsic force, operating independently of every external stimulus, into a great and successful future.

The following figures show the rapidity with which the population has increased from its very earliest beginnings to the present year:

INCREASE OF POPULATION.

YEAR.	AUTHORITY.	NUMBER.
1850.......	....	none
1860.......	U. S. Census	5,809
1870.......	" "	13,066
1880.......	" "	46,867
1883........	Directory estimates........................	91,337

The immense increase in numbers since the census of 1880, resting as it does upon unofficial authority, may naturally give rise to some question of the accuracy of the statement.

Yet, marvelous as they seem, the facts are well substantiated, and the figures are the result of the most moderate calculation. For several years past the city directory has been compiled by the same careful hands; the names it has taken have been strictly confined to those adults engaged in actual business or professional callings, and no exaggeration of numbers has been permitted. The above estimate of the city's population at the present time is obtained from the latest issue of the directory in the following manner: A proportional ratio has been determined between the directory total of 1880 and the population by census of that year. This ratio is 2.64, and upon this basis the population of each succeeding year has been calculated. A steady and slightly increasing gain in 1881, '82 and '83 has brought the population up to its present estimate. In this way, multiplying the number of the present directory names, 35,355, by $2\frac{64}{100}$, the above total of 94,337 is obtained.

THE WHEAT MARKET OF MINNEAPOLIS.

HE wheat market of Minneapolis, by a steady yearly increase, keeping pace with the development of the country tributary to it, transacts, at the present time, a larger aggregate of actual business than any city in America, with the single exception of New York. She is already the largest spring wheat center in the country, and reduces to flour the greatest quantity of grain.

Her trade in this cereal, unlike that of Chicago and other cities, is strictly legitimate.

Thus, of the 18,947,500 bushels received in 1882, but 2,005,000 bushels were re-shipped, whilst the remaining 16,942,500 bushels were turned into flour.

Whilst wheat is the chief staple of the Minneapolis grain market, the trade in other forms of grain has shown a corresponding increase.

In 1882 the city received 1,054,000 bushels of corn, an increase of 745,-000 bushels over the total of the preceding year; and 1,446,000 bushels of oats, against 420,800 bushels in 1881.

The aggregate of the whole grain trade for the last year was $23,500,000.

Not only the quantity but the quality of the wheat which, in the main, she reduces to flour, insures the destiny of Minneapolis as the principal wheat market of the Northwest.

The following tables will afford new evidence of the remarkable progress of the city, and of the possibilities of growth still open to her in the near future:

MONTHLY STATEMENT OF RECEIPTS OF WHEAT FOR SEVEN YEARS.

MONTHS.	1882.	1881.	1880.	1879.	1878.	1877.	1876.
January	1,297,000	1,235,700	822,300	197,470	128,800	233,200	258,625
February	1,431,000	965,000	485,600	492,102	477,600	155,600	253,125
March	1,079,500	1,151,710	541,460	595,556	332,440	126,889	376,875
April	876,500	1,057,500	580,100	199,810	512,000	393,600	597,875
May	1,125,500	1,552,550	811,300	599,526	386,400	178,440	331,875
June	1,133,100	1,653,300	761,360	598,984	288,600	833,200	552,750
July	1,011,000	1,185,450	923,600	640,940	266,000	366,100	388,500
August	1,031,500	1,201,500	672,800	455,713	210,800	176,200	267,200
September	2,552,000	1,512,000	696,280	540,570	250,000	426,100	410,625
October	2,629,500	1,989,050	1,390,700	976,611	416,800	666,400	571,350
November	2,469,000	1,718,250	1,588,280	886,190	602,800	566,100	570,375
December	2,282,000	1,311,950	1,042,290	770,302	168,100	588,000	453,000
Total	18,947,500	16,317,250	10,264,000	7,514,361	4,591,050	4,500,000	5,437,575

MONTHLY STATEMENT OF SHIPMENTS OF WHEAT FOR SEVEN YEARS.

MONTHS.	1882.	1881.	1880.	1879.	1878.	1877.	1876.
January	240,500	3,150	17,200	39,600	16,000	....	1,500
February	284,500	1,500	2,100	53,800	2,000	....	2,500
March	229,000	7,650	6,400	16,800	5,600	....	1,125
April	89,000	9,900	1,200	8,000	3,600	....	2,750
May	113,500	19,350	4,800	15,200	86,000	3,000	3,395
June	168,500	32,850	8,000	9,200	800	800	7,500
July	161,000	21,700	12,100	8,400	6,000	1,800	8,100
August	155,500	27,900	400	4,400	....	400	5,595
September	127,000	21,600	2,100	2,000	5,200	....	8,420
October	117,500	77,850	10,400	800	7,200	2,000	5,625
November	193,000	86,100	61,400	8,400	28,800	5,600	1,500
December	220,000	198,100	3,600	10,800	48,100	7,200	....
Total	2,105,000	514,750	133,600	177,100	195,200	20,200	48,039

MONTHLY STATEMENT OF RECEIPTS OF FLOUR FOR SEVEN YEARS.

MONTHS.	1882.	1881.	1880.	1879.	1878.	1877.	1876.
January	21,125	26,505	6,600	10,900	1,900	500	2,500
February	13,875	11,800	5,100	1,000	1,700	500	3,500
March	8,125	10,400	6,200	12,600	1,500	1,500	4,500
April	6,000	10,900	6,100	6,700	2,700	2,700	2,600
May	10,875	20,800	5,100	12,400	4,900	3,400	4,200
June	7,625	26,000	2,600	10,600	6,100	2,600	4,300
July	7,125	18,700	3,100	11,800	8,600	2,600	4,400
August	10,625	25,100	2,000	15,800	4,800	1,000	2,100
September	11,498	21,800	4,800	7,700	7,800	3,400	2,500
October	29,215	27,700	15,200	9,900	9,400	4,800	4,300
November	37,751	36,200	16,700	9,400	9,100	6,500	4,400
December	10,750	26,600	26,200	13,100	15,800	3,800	2,500
Total	210,498	262,500	103,000	130,900	64,300	33,200	41,390

MONTHLY STATEMENT OF SHIPMENTS OF FLOUR FOR SEVEN YEARS.

MONTHS.	1882.	1881.	1880.	1879.	1878.	1877.	1876.
January	207,790	211,192	93,116	74,260	81,130	41,650	57,350
February	180,122	158,180	81,238	86,090	80,114	18,696	49,300
March	162,215	220,431	139,900	169,506	95,801	42,150	77,200
April	169,577	269,440	136,100	105,713	112,632	83,350	70,800
May	200,639	289,838	159,116	130,611	61,650	92,770	86,300
June	141,997	312,627	171,156	131,518	63,983	67,650	99,900
July	161,552	309,632	189,923	117,716	65,239	70,880	82,200
August	202,667	307,115	190,227	137,070	11,250	62,575	83,800
September	288,237	293,350	112,107	118,686	62,258	78,825	91,500
October	495,088	386,005	253,011	174,413	87,900	128,800	112,000
November	492,615	204,390	237,338	186,121	88,189	117,027	106,600
December	166,453	163,173	252,375	166,565	91,631	131,591	83,726
Total	3,175,910	3,112,674	2,051,810	1,551,789	910,786	935,514	1,000,676

THE MANUFACTURE OF FLOUR.

THE flouring mills of Minneapolis are the possibilities of the water-fall made real; the material results of the matchless power which has borne so large a part in determining the prosperity of the city.

The multiplication of these manufactories, representing an immense investment of capital, the improvement of the process of reduction, and the quality of the wheat from which it is produced, have united to place Minneapolis far beyond any possible rivalry as a flour-milling center.

In 1863 only five mills were in operation, and 35,000 barrels of flour was considered a large annual yield; to-day twenty-seven establishments are running with an aggregate producing capacity, *per diem*, of 27,650 barrels.

In 1861, the mills produced 3,142,974 barrels of flour, and in 1882, in despite of the failure of early crops, only a little less than that number.

Of the product of 1882, over one-third was shipped direct to foreign markets, which were opened only three years ago to Minneapolis flour; 75,000 barrels were used for home consumption; and the remainder was sent to other domestic markets.

The statement appended shows the rate of increase during the period above named, though still but a small percentage of the growth possible within the easily available limits of the water-power.

REPORT OF FLOUR MANUFACTURE AND EXPORT FOR TWENTY-TWO YEARS.

YEAR.	PRODUCT. (bbls.)	FOREIGN EXPORT. (bbls.)
1860	30,000	
1865	98,000	
1870	193,000	
1873	585,000	
1874	727,000	
1875	843,000	
1876	1,000,675	
1877	935,544	
1878	910,786	109,183
1879	1,551,789	442,598
1880	2,051,840	769,442
1881	3,112,974	1,181,322
1882	3,124,919	

The city contains seven grain elevators which, together with the mills, possess a storage capacity of 4,340,000 bushels.

THE LUMBER MILLS.

HE lumber trade of 1850 was the first fruit gathered from the utilization of the water-power, and for many years was the chief industry of the cities of Minneapolis and St. Anthony.

From the first saw-mill, built by Mr. Franklin Steele in 1848, with its modest outfit and slender yield, to the seventeen large establishments of 1883 with a last year's manufacture of 312,239,000 feet, is a long and almost incredible step.

At the present time, the milling of lumber is only second in importance to the milling of flour, and is a witness not only to the development of the general manufacturing interests of Minneapolis, but also to the marvellous extent to which its own upbuilding has been carried.

An abundance of logs, a brisk demand both at home and abroad, and well sustained prices united to render the lumber season of 1882 unusually profitable.   The excess of sales over these of the preceding year, was nearly 78,000,000 feet, and nearly 200,000,000 feet were purchased for home use.

In consequence of this enormous home consumption the outside trade was supplied from other points, and there was a marked decrease, therefore, in the quantity usually shipped elsewhere.

The prospects for the lumber interest during the current year are unusually good.   With an even larger supply than ever before of raw material, with the anticipated addition of two new mills to the power already employed, and a constant demand in excess of the possibilities of supply, there is every reason to expect a growth corresponding to that of the preceding year.

The annual lumber production in the Minneapolis mills for the last thirteen years is appended in tabular form.

PRODUCTION OF LUMBER FOR 13 YEARS.

Year.	Feet.
1870	118,223,100
1871	117,157,000
1872	167,913,820
1873	189,910,000
1874	191,305,080
1875	156,055,000
1876	200,371,250
1877	120,676,000
1878	130,274,100
1879	140,154,500
1880	195,452,200
1881	230,403,000
1882	312,239,000

GENERAL MANUFACTURES.

A manufacturing basis is undoubtedly the firmest foundation upon which a city can be built, and the actual conditions which contribute to the possibility of its possession are the surest guarantee of a great future.

Granted these advantages to a new community, and every other form of human activity will be inevitably attracted to the spot. The development of these interests may be slow, but is accomplished in obedience to the law of supply answering to a persistent demand.

To say that Minneapolis rests upon so enviably secure a footing, is not, by any means, to assert that she has yet realized or fulfilled her destiny. Not only are many of her subordinate enterprises still in embryo, but even the fullness of her future as a manufacturing center is not yet apparent.

The power which drives her mill-wheels expends but a small proportion of itself upon the tasks to which it is already set. Four-fifths of the restless energy of the water-fall still runs to waste.

Large opportunities are still open, not merely to the flour and the saw-mill, but to every form of manufacture conducted by water or by steam.

The day cannot be far distant when the aggregate of the miscellaneous products of Minneapolis factories will far exceed the combined totals of these now predominant interests. Already a great number and variety of establishments have found place for themselves and market for their goods. Agricultural and general machinery, cars, furniture, hardware and stoves, wagons and carriages, sashes and doors, bricks, mill furnishings, barrels, harness, clothing, boots and shoes, crackers, cigars and beer, are articles of home production, on a large scale; and ere long Minneapolis will be a general manufacturing center for "the new Northwest."

In the year 1882, 7,388 men were employed within the limits of the city in the production of these miscellaneous articles to the amount of $17,000,000.

The total of manufactures, including flour and lumber, reached $43,-759,490, showing an increase, despite the partial failure of the wheat crop of 1881, over the preceeding year of $2,066,134.

The following is a summary of

MANUFACTURES FOR 1882:

MANUFACTURE.	Men Employed	Value of Manufacture.
Agricultural machinery	500	$1,480,000
Awnings, duck goods, etc.	90	140,000
Bags	30	225,000
Barrels and barrel stock	960	2,140,000
Beer	100	536,000
Blank Books, etc.	45	20,000
Boots and Shoes	200	515,000
Boxes, paper and wooden	30	52,000
Bread, crackers, etc.	136	115,000
Brick, stone, lime, etc.	140	220,000
Brooms and makers' supplies	23	48,000
Candies and confections	60	100,000
Cars	1300	1,870,000
Cigars	94	157,200
Clothing, cotton goods, etc.	454	784,800
Extracts, spices, etc.	32	220,000
Flour	1200	19,718,249
Furniture, beds, bed springs, etc.	320	908,000
Furs	20	31,000
Galvanized iron, roofing, etc.	108	12,000
Gloves and mittens	20	16,500
Hardware goods, stoves, etc.	60	200,500
Harness, saddlery, etc.	57	178,250
Lemon beer, etc.	10	51,000
Lumber	500	4,998,800
Machinery, castings, etc.	650	1,632,000
Marble and granite	18	186,000
Mill furnishers and builders	112	826,990
Millinery and hair goods	13	33,000
Oils and Paints	20	429,500
Paper	105	275,000
Picture frames, show cases, etc.	60	170,000
Printing (job), lithographing, etc.	125	275,000
Sash, doors, etc.	1200	2,030,000
Shirts	41	121,000
Soap, glue, etc.	85	419,000
Tinware	35	115,000
Wagons, carriages, etc.	150	319,000
Woodwork (miscellaneous)	90	275,000
Woolen goods (North Star Mill)	220	482,000
Miscellaneous	480	605,000
Totals	**9,912**	**$43,759,490**

PILLSBURY 'A' MILL.—Capacity, 5,000 barrels daily.

5

(65)

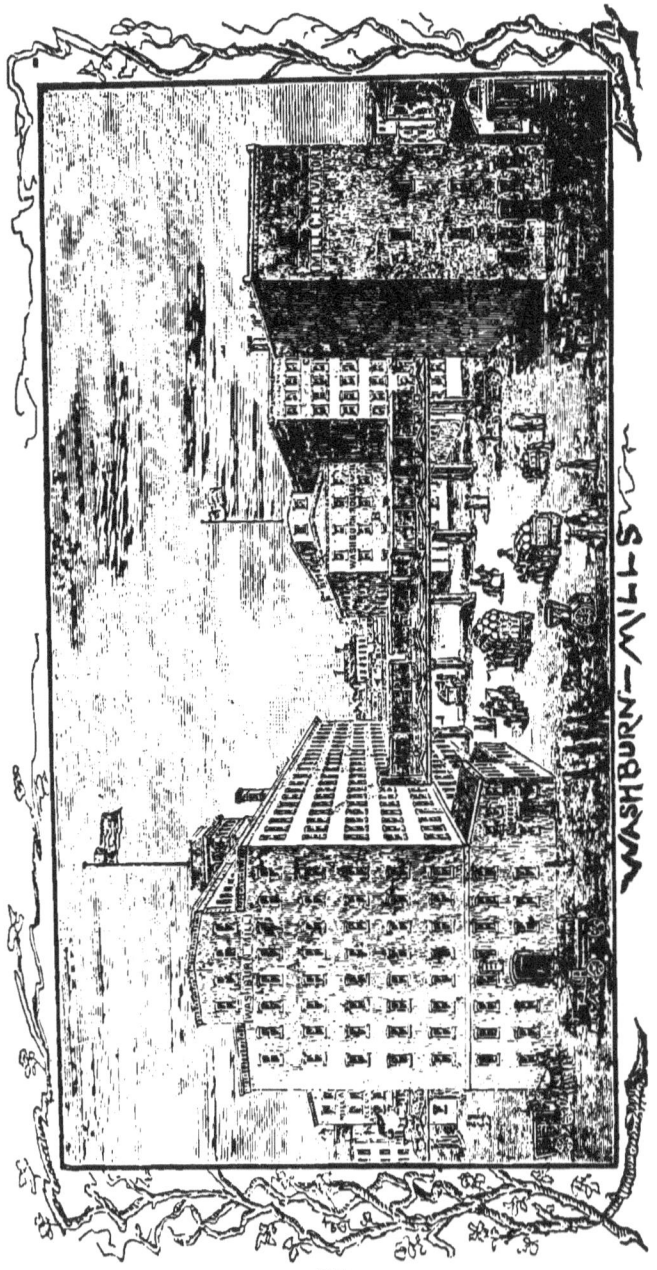

WASHBURN-MILLS

WHOLESALE AND RETAIL TRADE.

ECOND only to the remarkable progress of the manufacturing interests of Minneapolis has been the history of her growth in trade. As the railroad center of a large tributary country, and the chief market for its agricultural products, it was necessary that the city should become a wholesale depot for general merchandise.

The increase of jobbing trade has been of comparatively recent date, and of natural order ; a steady, healthy growth in direct proportion to the demand of neighboring custom.

The pre-eminence of its manufacturing position has, perhaps, tended to obscure the fact of its great commercial importance; a fact which every year, forces itself more markedly upon public recognition.

Seven years since, the aggregate of wholesale trade transacted during the year was $5,373,651; in 1882 it reached the sum of $97,000,000;—a result which surpasses the most glowing expectations of success.

New capital is continually seeking investment in the city, and the establishment of new jobbing firms is only embarrassed by a lack of suitable store-buildings.

There can be no question that Minneapolis and her sister city are rapidly drawing away from Chicago the trade of all the extreme northwest of the country of which they are natural business centers, and as this new country develops its resources the wholesale trade must assume proportions compared with which its present is insignificant. The appended summary gives the aggregates of jobbing business in the various departments, for the year 1882.

Agricultural Machinery	$ 6,985,000
Awnings, duck goods, etc	208,000
Bags	180,000
Barrels and barrel stock	2,110,000
Beer, liquors, etc	1,850,000
Boxes, paper and wooden	50,000
Bread, crackers, etc	168,000
Brooms	120,000
Boots and shoes	950,000
Carpets	42,000
Cigars and tobacco	510,000
Clothing	335,000
Candies and confectionery	320,000
Dry Goods	3,107,000
Drugs	600,000
Earthenware, etc	357,000
Extracts, spices, etc	255,000
Flour	19,500,000
Fuel	1,000,000

SYNDICATE BLOCK.—330x165 ; seven acres of floorage.

Furniture	$380,000
Furs	17,000
Galvanized iron, etc	204,000
Gloves and mittens	20,000
Grain, commission, etc	25,750,000
Groceries	8,200,000
Guns, revolvers, etc	36,000
Hardware	2,055,500
Harness, saddlery, etc	494,000
Hides, pelts, etc	303,000
Jewelry	261,000
Lemon beer, etc	55,000
Live stock	2,900,000
Lumber, lath and shingles	4,900,000
Machinery, castings, etc	2,160,000
Meat, fish, etc	875,000
Millinery and hair goods	115,500
Oils and paints	490,000
Paper	645,000
Picture Frames, show cases, etc	165,000
Produce, feed and commission	3,510,000
Rubber goods	140,000
Sash, doors, etc	1,300,000
Shirts	60,000
Soap, glue, etc	470,000
Stationery	60,000
Tinware	110,000
Toys	56,000
Wagons, carriages, etc	110,000
Wall paper	22,000
Waste paper, rags, etc	290,000
Woolen goods	420,000
Miscellaneous	1,400,000

Total for 1882	$97,376,000
Total for 1881	83,501,984
Increase for the year	$13,874,016

REAL ESTATE.

HE unprecedented activity in the realty-market, which has especially characterized the last two years of the city's history, has been a subject for no little wonder to many.

The large number of transfers made, and the constantly rising prices of property, have excited a natural question of its legitimate character ; but, after making due allowance for any speculative element in the case, there is still a wonderful margin of growth, which can only be accounted for upon the ground of the rapid influx of people and capital and the increased call for residences, business offices and stores.

Placed side by side with the development of manufacturing and trade interests, it will be seen that real estate has, for the most part, only kept pace with these, and that the number and consideration of the transfers effected are but the natural response to an importunate demand for property, especially in suburban portions of the city.

A comparison of the transactions of former years, with those of 1882, shows a remarkable rate of increase.

YEAR.	Deeds.	Consideration.
1880	3,096	$ 4,518,364
1881	4,366	7,393,428
1882	7,194	18,701,256
Increase in 1882 over 1881	2,828	$11,307,828

BUILDING IN MINNEAPOLIS.

THE best possible guarantee of the legitimacy of the real estate business in the city, is the correspondingly active demand for and the erection of residence and business buildings.

That this demand has been, and still is largely in excess of the supply is proved by the long continued difficulty in obtaining shelter for either goods or families.

Buildings of every description are habitually leased prior to their completion, and the scarcity is still apparent.

The extension of the city by new buildings is fairly uniform in every direction and the actual limits of the city already cover a very large area.

Many large business edifices have recently been completed and many more are now in process of construction. The Syndicate block and the Grand Opera House have been finished at a cost of half a million dollars; the Chamber of Commerce building is being erected and will cost, with ground, $225,000; the Milwaukee and St. Paul Railway is extending its car shops and works; a new postoffice is to be built by the government; the foundations of a magnificent Union depot, to be built below the suspension bridge, are being excavated; the West Hotel is rapidly progressing, and will cost, furnished, not far from $1,250,000. This superb hostelry will contain 400 rooms, will be entirely fire-proof throughout, and in elegance, convenience and completeness will be unsurpassed on the continent.

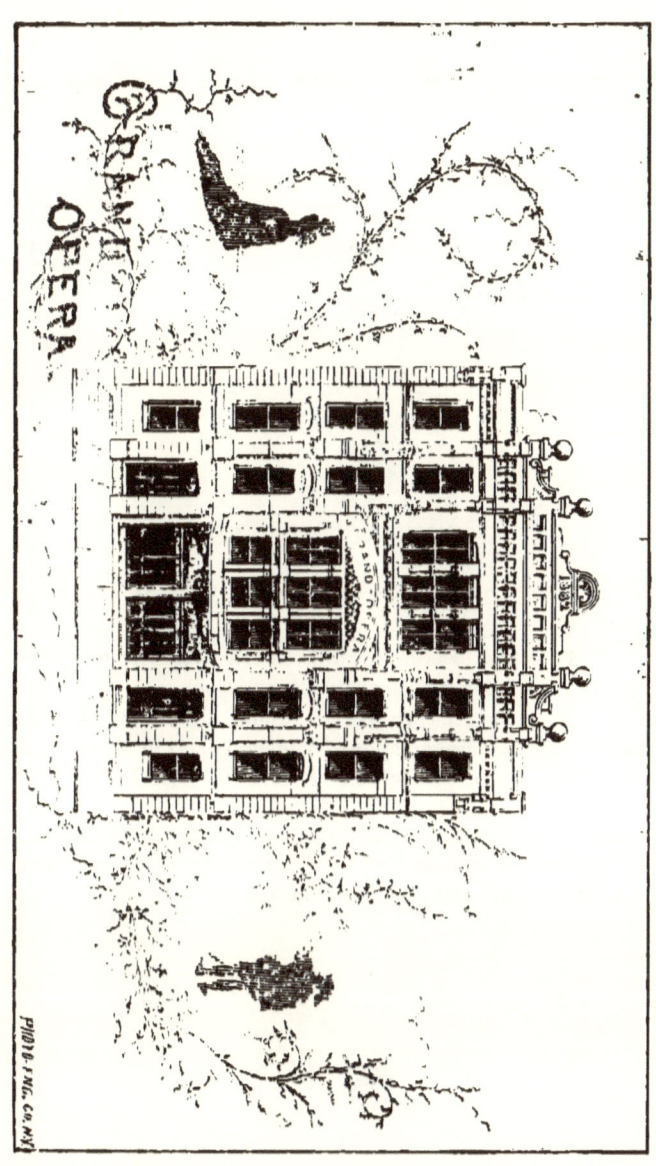

The comparative estimate which follows has been carefully compiled from accurate reports.

NEW BUILDINGS

New structures erected in 1881		2,210
" dwellings " 1882	2,208	
" business structures erected in 1882	310	
" mills and factories " "	41	
" warehouses and miscellaneous buildings in 1882	72	
		2,631
Estimated new structures in 1883		3,500
Cost of new buildings in 1882		$9,130,125
" " " " 1883 (estimated)		11,000,000

BANKING BUSINESS.

IGHT public banking institutions and three private bankers, are at present doing business in Minneapolis.

They have an aggregate capital of $3,500,000, and their operations in 1882 reached an approximate total of $150,000,000.

Since the first bank in Minneapolis was organized (A. D. 1855), twenty-four institutions have come into existence, but of these, thirteen have either been merged in other institutions or retired from business. The present number are instances of "the survival of the fittest," and rest upon a solid basis of capital and safe business.

THE NEW CHAMBER OF COMMERCE BUILDING.

THE CHAMBER OF COMMERCE AND THE BOARD OF TRADE.

THE Chamber of Commerce came into existence in October, 1881, and held its first meeting in November of that year. Its growth since that time is illustrative of the progress of the city.

Its original incorporators numbered 26, whilst its membership at the close of the first fiscal year was 536, and has since increased.

A fine building is now in process of construction, at Third street and

Fourth avenue south, to be occupied by the Chamber upon its completion. Its cost is estimated, with the realty, at $225,000.

The purposes of the corporation are: "To facilitate the buying and selling of all products, to inculcate principles of justice and equity in trade, to facilitate speedy adjustments of business disputes, to acquire and disseminate valuable commercial information, and, generally, to secure to its members the benefits of co-operation in the furtherance of their legitimate business pursuits, and to advance the general prosperity and business interests of the city of Minneapolis."

The Board of Trade, whose membership is largely identical with that of the Chamber of Commerce, is not a commercial body in the usual sense. Its sole purpose is to promote the material prosperity of Minneapolis by proposing and encouraging public measures calculated to add to the growth of the city, enlarge the field of its trade and enhance its general welfare. To this organization is due much of that harmony and vigor of action which characterize the business community of Minneapolis when any question of public improvement or local advantage is under consideration. Its membership numbers about two hundred.

RAILWAY SYSTEMS CENTERING IN MINNEAPOLIS.

THE first indication of a city's permanent growth is its inclusion among the number of places with which one or more important railway lines communicate; and the final recognition of its established greatness is the concentration of railway systems towards it as a terminal point, and a traffic producing center. In the present case, both these indications have been fulfilled. In earlier pages the extension of railroads within the State of Minnesota has already been enlarged upon, and the reader is therefore familiar with the present status of the companies whose iron roads traverse the country surrounding the city of Minneapolis. A glance at the State map will show the position which Minneapolis occupies as the heart from which these great arteries of commerce diverge, and towards which their returning currents of trade tend. These diverging and constantly extending lines are the radii of the agricultural and commercial area which the city commands. Along these courses of travel come in the raw supplies which feed her manufactories, and go out the finished products of her trade and industry.

By virtue of her natural position, and by means of these great avenues, she has unchangeably become the depot for the collection of the agricultural resources of a practically unlimited area, or the medium through which they pass; as well as the main ultimate point of distribution for the commodities which its rapidly increasing population demands. A hint is furnished by the fact, that one point of a compass being placed at Minneapolis and the other at New Orleans, and the latter being swung around to the west and northwest, it will describe a line which does not reach the outer circle of fertile, growing country, lying beyond Minneapolis, which, by reason of her geographical situation and extensive railway system, she must naturally and permanently control. Nineteen distinct railways thus concentrate their trains and traffic at Minneapolis, either over their own independent roadways or, by arrangement, over other stem lines entering the city. Sixteen of these reach Minneapolis with their own rails. The list is as follows:

ST. PAUL, MINNEAPOLIS & MANITOBA: Main Line, St. Paul Short Line, St. Cloud & Fargo Line, Breckenridge Line, Lake Minnetonka Line. 1,314 miles.

CHICAGO, MILWAUKEE & ST. PAUL: Main Line, Fort Snelling Line, St. Paul Short Line, Iowa & Minnesota Division, Hastings & Dakota Division. 4,383 miles.

MINNEAPOLIS & ST. LOUIS RAILWAY: Main Line, Minnetonka Line, Stillwater Line. 424 miles.

CHICAGO, ROCK ISLAND & PACIFIC. Over M. & St. L. R. R.

CHICAGO, ST. PAUL, MINNEAPOLIS & OMAHA. 1,257 miles.

CHICAGO & NORTHWESTERN. Over Omaha Line. 3,489 miles.

NORTHERN PACIFIC RAILRORD: Main Line. 2,100 miles.

MINNEAPOLIS, LYNDALE & MINNETONKA RAILROAD. 22 miles.

These are operated by eight separate corporations. They send out from the city over one hundred passenger trains daily, and here originate more than 230,000 car loads of freight traffic yearly. Their recent rate of extension has been more rapid than that of railways traversing any other section of the country, and one of them has a greater mileage than any company in the United States.

So closely are these corporations allied to the commercial and manufacturing interests of the city, that it is worth while to speak briefly of each.

THE CHICAGO, MILWAUKEE AND ST. PAUL COMPANY.—
Although the name of Minneapolis is not incorporated in that of the
company in question, this city is its terminal point upon five divisions
or lines.   These are known as the Main Line, St. Paul Short Line, Fort
Snelling Line, Iowa and Minnesota Division, and Hastings and Dakota
Division.

THE UNION DEPOT. (IN PROCESS OF ERECTION.)

Its connections with the city have been further strengthened by the
erection here during the last season of large car-shops, at a cost of $500,000,
which constitute the main plant for the company's repairing and manufacturing west of the Mississippi; and wherein not less than 2,000 men will
be employed.

Its policy is one of extension, as rapidly as genuine western enterprise,
combined with safe and conservative management, warrants.

THE ST. PAUL, MINNEAPOLIS & MANITOBA RAILWAY COM-
PANY.—Three of the four main lines of this company's road terminate in
Minneapolis. New freight houses, suitable for the accommodation of its
fast growing business, are to be immediately erected here; its short double-
track line to Lake Minnetonka is completed; and its main lines are being
rapidly extended.

A large addition to its total of mileage has been made during the last
year. It opens up to the city a vast region, including the Red River Valley, of richly productive country.

Under the auspices of this company, the associated railroads are constructing a fine stone-arch viaduct across the Mississippi at the Falls of
St. Anthony, and laying the foundations of a Union Passenger Depot
at the foot of the suspension bridge, both of which will add alike
to the railway interests and to the architectural beauty of the city.
Not less than $2,000,000 will be expended upon these colossal improve-
ments.

THE MINNEAPOLIS AND ST. LOUIS RAILWAY COMPANY.—
The road owned by this company is operated in conjunction with the
Chicago and Rock Island railway as a through line to Chicago. Its ter-
minus, as well as its general offices and car-shops are in this city.

It has undergone some recent extension in the direction of a point
opposite Redwood Falls, on the Minnesota river, and thereby renders a
new section of country tributary to Minneapolis. In addition, the line has
instituted some general improvement in the character of its accomodations.

CHICAGO, ST. PAUL, MINNEAPOLIS AND OMAHA RAILWAY.
—The recent change of ownership which has transferred the control of
this road to the hands of the CHICAGO AND NORTHWESTERN RAILWAY has
brought the latter into more intimate and mutually beneficial connection
with Minneapolis.

It is to be fairly expected that the added impetus given to both roads
by their practical identification will be fruitful of better management,
greater enterpise, and improved accomodations for the traveling public, and
means the placing of Minneapolis upon an equal standing with other
points in its relations with this important railway system.

THE ST. PAUL AND DULUTH RAILWAY COMPANY.—The
connection of this system with Minneapolis is very close, although
its terminus is not in this city.

With an addition of only thirteen miles of track during the past year.
it has experienced an increase of sixty per cent. in its freight shipments.
and of sixty-five per cent. in its passenger travel.

Improvements of the road and its accomodations projected during the last season are reported at a cost of $600,000.

THE NORTHERN PACIFIC RAILWAY COMPANY.—The completion of this gigantic enterprise, now practically accomplished, marks a notable epoch in the railway history of the world, and not less in the annals of this country's material development and progress. This latest and greatest of the transcontinental lines has its western termini at Portland, Oregon, where it is met by the tidewater navigation of the Columbia river, and at New Tacoma, on Puget Sound, Washington territory, where it reaches the water of the Pacific ocean proper.

On the east, one arm touches the head of Lake Superior, and thence follows the south shore eastward to the Michigan boundary, while the other and principal arm has its terminus in Minneapolis, with running arrangements which carry its trains on to St. Paul.

The construction of this highway opens and renders accessible to Minneapolis a fertile tributary country extending 1,200 miles north and west. Minneapolis, as the first great city reached by the Northern Pacific Railroad in its progress from the Pacific ocean, naturally and necessarily receives the chief impetus resulting from this great work, and enjoys a larger advantage than any other city from the trade this thoroughfare is developing.

The Northern Pacific Company is now constructing this main southeastern arm down the east bank of the Mississippi river to Minneapolis, the crossing to be made to the west bank over a substantial double-track iron bridge, now building, within the city limits, near Twenty-sixth Avenue North. The company has recently purchased nearly one hundred and fifty acres of ground, for terminal purposes, within the city, and will expend several million dollars here, in such buildings and improvements as will be adequate to handle its immense traffic at this point.

The fact that Minneapolis now is, and will permanently continue to be, the market for the bulk of the grain crop produced in the fertile belt traversed by the Northern Pacific Railroad, and the chief distributing and shipping point for those manufactured commodities which are naturally sent in return to the people of the grain-producing region, renders the relations of this city to the road in question particularly intimate and important.

THE MINNEAPOLIS, LYNDALE & MINNETONKA RAILWAY. —Seeing that the main stations of this road are either within the limits of the city or are dependent upon it for their importance, the line may be regarded fairly, and without detriment to itself or detraction from its usefulness. as a suburban railway.

The road has been in operation four years, extending first to Lake Calhoun, later to Lake Harriet, and subsequently to Lake Minnetonka. Its further terminus is at Excelsior, a small town on the borders of the last mentioned lake.

It has exercised a very important influence in the encouragement of building in the outlying portions of the city, adjacent to its track, placing a means of transit within the reach of residents who are distant from their places of business, without which such settlement would have been greatly retarded.

––––––

When the early history of railroads as related to Minneapolis is considered, when it is remembered that prior to 1862 no railway existed in the State, that for two years subsequent to that date only ten miles of line were in operation between, St. Anthony and St. Paul, and that it was not until 1867 that a track first entered the Minneapolis proper of that period, —this record of the present general determination of railway systems toward the city, becomes one of most remarkable import.

It signifies,—in common with the preceding facts of population, extending area, trade, and manufacture,—that not only has a great city developed from the nucleus of the water-fall, but that Fate with " the forefinger of all time " points to her as the present and permanent metropolis of " the new Northwest."

THE UNIVERSITY OF MINNESOTA

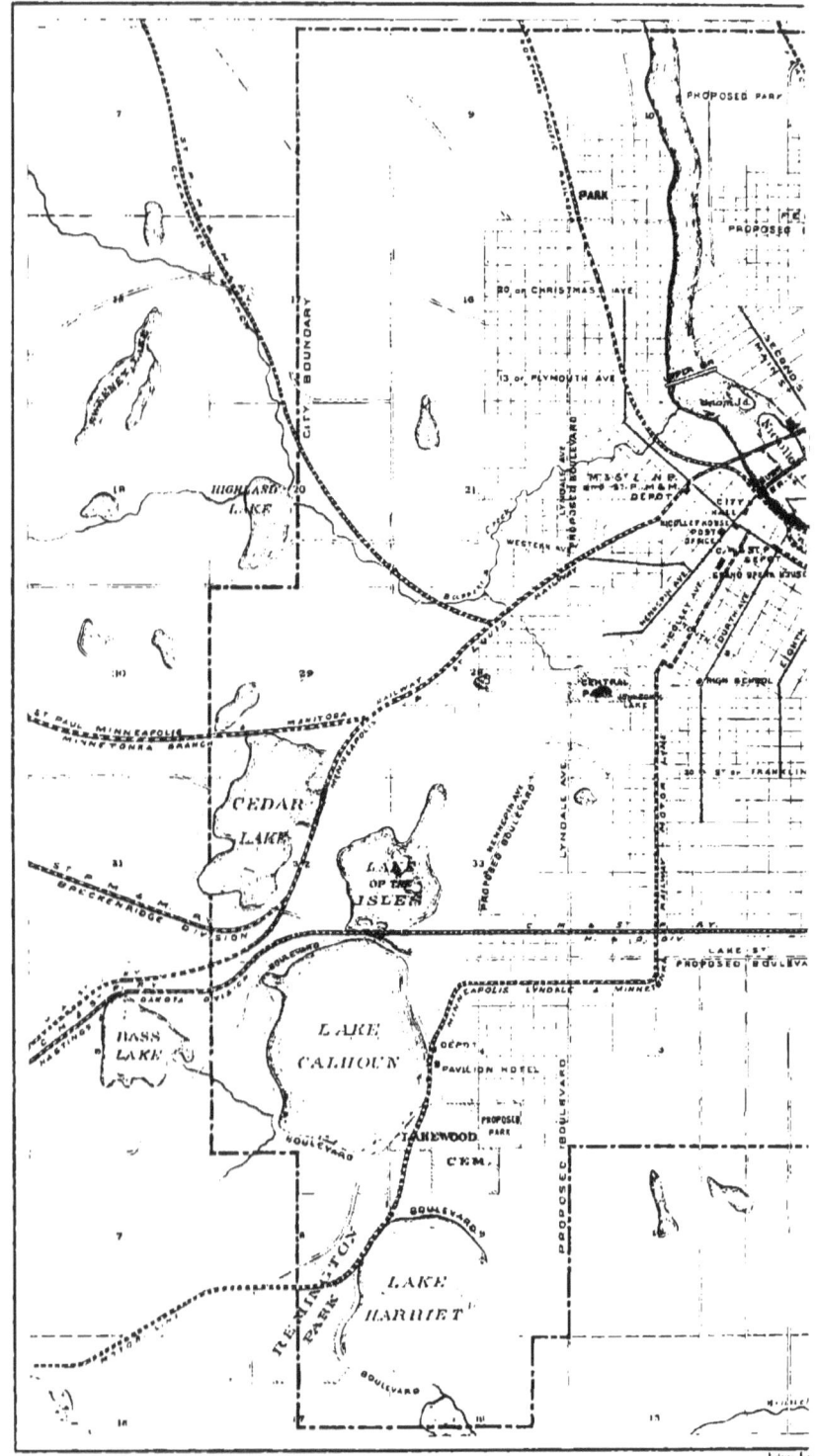

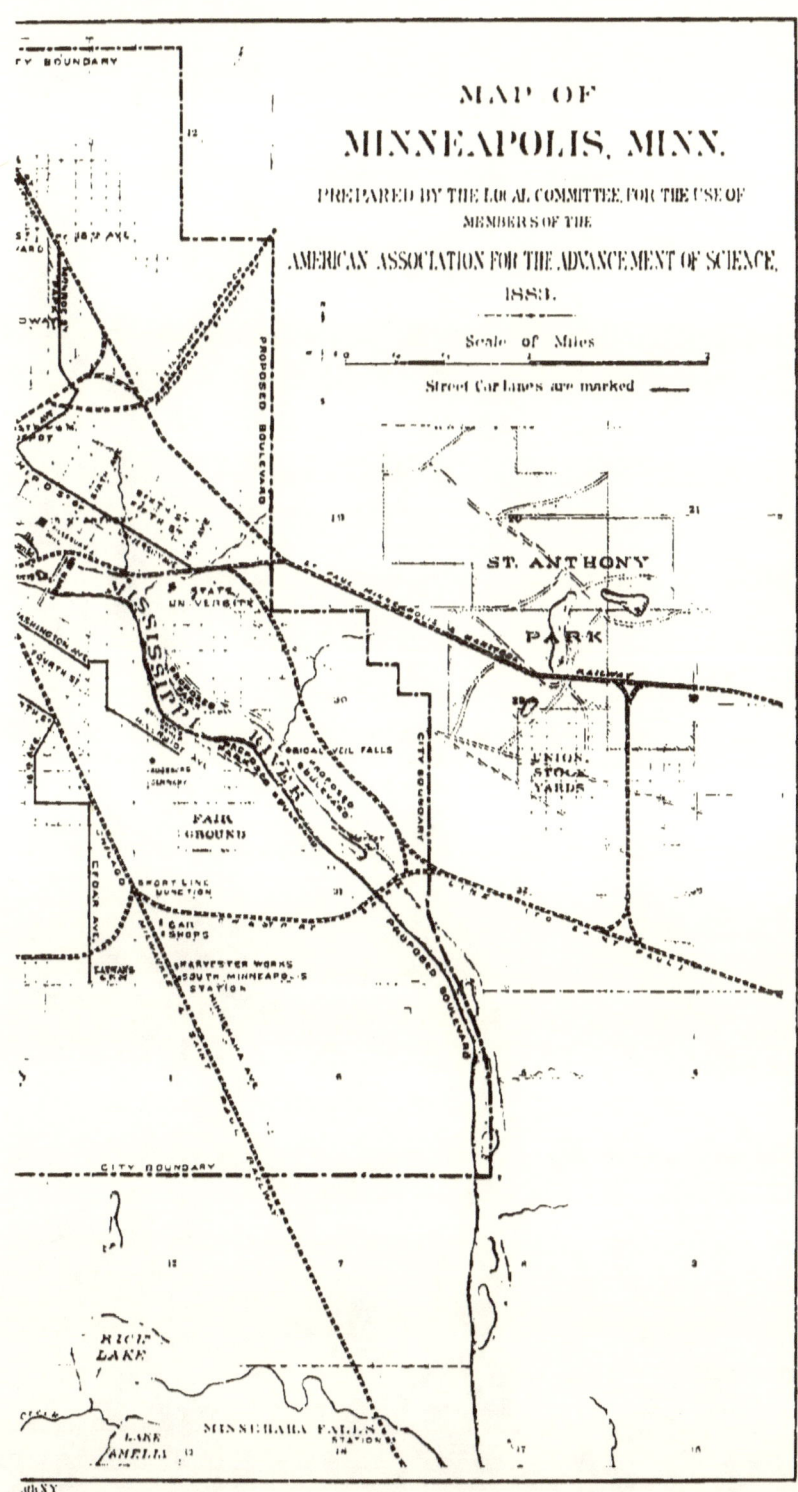

THE
PRINCIPAL FEATURES

OF THE

City of Minneapolis.

— - —

HE preceding chapters have been devoted to a review, in brief, of those great interests, which are always of vital importance in the upbuilding of a city, and whose growth has marked the onward progress of Minneapolis to her present secure position. In the pages which follow, we shall, in like manner, sketch the principal features of the present city, with especial reference to the economic improvements she has projected, and to the intellectual and social refinement she has attained.

Wealth may be the measure of a city's commercial importance, but it does not fairly gauge the well-being of her people.

Their real welfare is conditioned upon the safe-guards which she throws around their moral and physical health, and upon the perfection of those institutions which foster the cultivation of mental, moral, physical, and social integrity.

That Minneapolis, despite of her rapid and recent growth, is exceptionally well endowed in these respects, needs no other demonstration than is afforded by the following brief description of her public works, protective agencies, educational interests, and literary, scientific, musical, charitable and church societies.

MINNEAPOLIS STREET SYSTEM.

IN laying out the streets and avenues of Minneapolis engineering skill has had to contend, in some measure, with the inequalities of nature.

The river which contributes largely to its natural beauty, at the same time mars the symmetry of the city. Its deviating course makes it practically impossible to adhere strictly to the system of rectangular lines which is acknowledged to be the model of convenience in the arrangement of a town. On each side of the river, for a space about a mile in width, from the upper bridge to the line of the State University, the streets are laid out in a direction diagonal to the points of the compass; but with the exception of this area, the plan of the city is uniform, most of the avenues running north and south, and the streets east and west. The streets are named numerically, with few exceptions, and are numbered on the plan of a hundred numbers to each block. The accompanying map will serve as an illustration of this general arrangement and as a miniature guide to the city. Extensive plans are being made or are now in process of execution for the improvement of the street-system in general.

Several roadways are being graded to the proper level, and 20,000 yards of paving has been or will be laid during the current year, partly in granite and partly in cedar blocks.

The streets are lighted by gas, and in the centre of the city, by means of an immense iron mast, 257 feet in height, bearing upon it eight electric lights, with an aggregate of 32,000 candle-power.

This light-mast illuminates a wide area surrounding it. It is similar to those used in the city of Cleveland, and is supplied with power from a single dynamo machine by the Minnesota Brush Electric Company.

The Minneapolis Street Railway Company has already a large system of lines and is constantly extending its tracks in every direction as the needs of newly settled districts require. About twenty miles of new trackage have been laid during the past year, at an expense, including minor improvements, of $225,000.

A table of the various lines and their terminal points will be appended to this volume.

Stone arch viaduct for railway use at St. Anthony Falls; 2310 feet in length; 65 feet above water level

BRIDGES.

HE growth of business, and the consequently more intimate relations established between the east and the west sides of the river, together with the rapid extension of the city, have necessitated the construction of several bridges, not only over the Mississippi, but also over some of the main thoroughfares where they are intersected by railroads.

The great suspension bridge crossing the river from Bridge Square on the West Side to Nicollet Island, has few equals either for strength or beauty. It was built in 1876 at a cost of $221,024.50.

The length of the bridge-way is 630 feet, and the towers are eighty feet in height.

The total strength of the cables, the largest of which are nine inches in diameter, is 10,995,072 pounds, while the total breaking strain of the bridge is estimated at 4,980,000 pounds.

The upper and lower bridges were built in 1874. The new Plymouth Avenue bridge was erected in 1882, and also one on Lyndale Avenue over Bassett's creek; the two requiring an expenditure of $72,000.

The railroad bridges crossing the Mississippi are that of the St. Paul, Minneapolis & Manitoba Railway at Nicollet Island, the Milwaukee "Short Line" bridge below Meeker Island, and the magnificent stone-arch viaduct now being thrown diagonally across the river at the Falls of St. Anthony, by the St. Paul, Minneapolis & Manitoba Company for the joint use of all roads centering here. This structure has a length of 2,300 feet, consisting of sixteen spans of eighty feet each, four spans of one hundred feet each and three spans of forty feet each. Its surface has a width of twenty-eight feet, intended to accommodate two parallel railway tracks, at a height of sixty-five feet above the water level. The piers are of granite and their foundations are in the native rock twenty feet below the surface. The remainder of the work is of magnesian limestone from quarries at Kasota, Minnesota, and the blue limestone which is taken from the local quarries in Minneapolis. This bridge is the longest of its kind in the United States, and will cost not far from $1,300,000.

In addition to these, the Northern Pacific Railway Company, as mentioned on an earlier page, has commenced work on a double-track iron railroad bridge at Twenty-fourth Avenue north, by means of which their tracks will cross to the west side of the river.

During the year, the St. Paul, Minneapolis & Manitoba Railroad, has built or completed a bridge over its tracks at Holden Street, Western Avenue, University Avenue, Fourth Street southeast, and Fourteenth Avenue southeast.

Their maintenance has now been assumed by the city government.

The exact location of all of these structures, with the exception of the projected Northern Pacific Railway bridge may be determined by reference to the map of Minneapolis, facing page 81.

CITY SEWER SYSTEM.

IT is inevitable that a city which has had a growth so unusually rapid as that of Minneapolis should suffer from the temporary inadequacy of certain general improvements and, especially, of its sewer-system.

To secure an efficient system of city-sewerage, requires an outlay of time and money which preclude the possibility of keeping pace in its construction with the rapid extension of residence area.

Minneapolis has suffered from this inadequacy for some time past, but is now putting forth active remedial efforts in her own behalf.

Much work has been done within the past year, and much more is now in hand, to provide the city with suitable water-mains, wells and tunnels.

Six or seven additional miles of sewerage will be completed before the winter sets in, and not many seasons will elapse before all the thickly-peopled portion of the city will have received the full benefit of these improvements.

Re-inforced by a sufficient water-supply, they must soon be fruitful of markedly beneficial results upon the already satisfactory health-statistics of the city.

CITY WATER SUPPLY.

INNEAPOLIS is furnished with water from the Mississippi river by means of four pumps worked by three Turbine water-wheels; the water being pumped directly through the mains to the houses of the consumers, on the Holly system.

The water-works are situated at the Falls, on the west bank of the river, and distribute water from thence, on both sides of the river, through twenty-four and three-fourths miles of main.

An immense supply of water is drawn from them daily, falling, in the summer season, little short of the full capacity of the pumps, which is estimated at thirteen million gallons.

The number of consumers during the year 1882, was 2,755; and 313 hydrants for fire purposes, 175 stop-gates, and 11 cisterns were in use.

Despite the recent addition of large pumping capacity, with two 500 horse-power wheels, the supply, under the test of any grave emergency is still inadequate.

Vigorous measures are needed, and are now being adopted, to insure an increase of power commensurate with the rapid extension of the city's limits and equal to any strain that may be put upon it in event of fire. The present daily pumping capacity will be increased by ten million gallons before November of the present year, and another ten million gallons early in 1884, making an aggregate of thirty-three million gallons.

Not only the *quantity*, but also the *quality* of the water supplied by the city has been a subject of debate, for which there is, at present, but slender cause.

Whilst the increase of the city's sewerage, pouring into the river, must prove, at no distant day, an actual source of pollution to the water, and and suggests the propriety of a further removal of the Works to a place of more assured safety than they, at present, occupy,—there is, as yet, no real ground for alarm.

Properly filtered, as all water should be which is intended for drinking-purposes, it is as pure as nine-tenths of the water of our lakes and rivers.

PUBLIC BUILDINGS.

THE excellence of architecture which characterizes many of the private blocks of the city cannot be said to have transferred itself, as yet, to the Public Buildings of Minneapolis.

THE CITY HALL stands facing Bridge Square at the point of convergence of Hennepin and Nicollet Avenues. It is a plain, massive structure, formed of Minneapolis lime-stone, four and five stories in height, with a tower and high mansard roof. It contains the offices or headquarters of the Mayor, the Chief of Police, the City Treasurer, the Comptroller, Clerk, Engineer, Physician, Park Commissioners and the Superintendents of the Water Works and of the Poor. The portions of the building not used by the city are mainly occupied by the Daily Minnesota Tribune, while the Western Union Telegraph Company, the Board of Trade and the Northwestern Telephone Exchange find quarters beneath its roof.

THE COURT HOUSE is situated on the corner of Eighth Avenue, South, and Third Street. It has long proved inadequate to the purpose for which it is used, and is now undergoing considerable enlargement. It holds all the county offices and law courts.

THE POST OFFICE at present occupies the corner portion of the great Boston Block, on the corner of Hennepin Avenue and Third St., completed about a year ago. This building is, in itself, a fine piece of architecture, but it is the result of private enterprise, and the Government holds only a limited tenure of its present quarters.

A few months since, a Commission, appointed by the Government, visited Minneapolis for the purpose of selecting a site for a permanent Post-office building. The ground selected lies at the corner of First Avenue, South, and Third Street, and plans have been drafted for the new structure, which will be commenced this year, an appropriation of $175,-000 having been made for the purpose. A cut of the proposed building is given elsewhere.

PARKS AND PUBLIC GROUNDS.

AT the last session of the Legislature, (1883), an act was passed appointing a Board of fifteen Park Commissioners for the city of Minneapolis, and the question of the purchase and improvement of park grounds being submitted to the vote of the people at the last election, a large majority declared in favor of the measure.

The city has, accordingly, authorized the issue of $550,000 of bonds for the purchase of property to be devoted to park purposes, and has also provided for a tax of one mill on each dollar of valuation of taxable property, the proceeds of which, aggregating, at present estimates, $50,000 per annum, are to be employed in the improvement of the same.

A special tax is to be levied upon the owners of real estate abutting upon park improvements, which will amount to not less than fifty per cent. of the total cost of the park property, and is to be applied to the park improvement fund.

Since its appointment, the board of commissioners has been actively engaged in the selection and purchase of several tracts of land, and in devising plans for an extensive system of parks and boulevards. The work that has been already done may be very briefly sketched, but it is the earnest of possessions in the near future of which the citizens of Minneapolis may well be proud.

The title has been acquired to a tract of thirty acres, lying between Hennepin Avenue and Yale Place, and between Oak Grove Street and Harmon Place, and including Johnson's Lake. This is to be known as *Central Park.*

In the northern division of the city, west of the river, about thirty acres have been substantially acquired, situated between Twenty-sixth and Twenty-ninth Avenues, North, and bounded on the west by Lyndale Avenue, and by Fifth street on the east. The park, as yet unnamed, will lie upon high wooded ground, overlooking the whole city.

On the east side of the river, twelve acres, bounded by Broadway on the south, Thirteenth Avenue, N. E., on the north, Jefferson Street on the west, and Monroe Street on the east, have been chosen for an East Minneapolis Park.

On the west bank of the river, twenty acres have been selected; adjoining the grounds of the Sisters' Hospital, on the south, and lying in the sixth ward. These are to be converted into a South Park.

In addition to these parks, situated in each natural division of the city, a magnificent system of boulevards will entirely surround Lake Calhoun and Lake Harriet; another grand boulevard will extend along the whole east bank of the river, from the State University grounds to the Ramsey County line; and a third will skirt the west bank of the river from the point where it is intersected by Washington Avenue, and will run thence through the South Park to Riverside Avenue.

Further to complete the chain of boulevards, it is proposed, but not yet finally determined, (1) to convert Lyndale Avenue into a park-way, extending from the North Park, and connecting by a short boulevard with the Lake Harriet system; (2) to lay out a system of boulevards on the east side, by which the river-chain will be linked to the East Park; and (3) to make a boulevard, in direct connection with that encircling the lakes, extending five miles down Lake Street to the river bank.

At the point where this road touches the river, the latter is enclosed by high bluffs, an island stands in the center of the stream, and on the opposite side is the terminal extremity of Marshall Street, running thence from St. Paul. Should the authorities of the latter city convert Marshall Street into a boulevard, a bridge can be thrown across from the island to either bank, (this being the most favorable point for it between Fort Snelling and the Falls of St. Anthony,) and a direct park-way be thus opened between Lake Calhoun in Minneapolis and the center of the City of St. Paul.

Irrespective of this possibility, however, the complete system of Minneapolis Parks and Boulevards—the former covering nearly a hundred acres and the latter about thirty miles in length—when perfectly laid out, will be incomparably the finest in America, and possibly without a rival in the world.

No larger or more varied combination of the elements of natural beauty can anywhere be found in the near neighborhood of a great city than are here grouped together. Nature has bestowed with lavish hand upon the environments of Minneapolis all her most picturesque forms of scenery, with the sole exception of great mountains. Rocks and streams, the cataract and the river, hills, and lakes, and woods, and a rich minor vegetation lend their attractions to her surroundings, and are destined to aid in forming the pleasure-grounds of her people.

Upon the city map, appended to this volume, are traced in outline these acquired and projected improvements.

MINNEAPOLIS FIRE DEPARTMENT.

— - —

THE latest report of the Chief of Department, F. L. Stetson, shows the command of a manual force of thirty-two permanent hands, and forty-three call-men. The latter are not required to remain on duty during the day, but help to make up the full night force between the hours of 9 P. M. and 6 A. M.

The Department has in use four steam fire engines, five two-horse hose carriages, one single-horse hose cart, two hook and ladder trucks, one two-horse chemical engine, and one supply wagon. In addition to these, one two-horse hose carriage, and three hand hose carts are employed as reserve reels. Thirty miles of fire alarm telegraph and fifty-three alarm boxes are in operation.

One hundred and four alarms have been turned in between March 1st and August 1st, 1883.

The total losses by fire for the year 1882, were estimated at $330,000, about four-fifths of which was covered by insurance.

The Department service is well organized, but its work is temporarily embarrassed by the deficiency of the City water supply. Theoretically, the pressure from the pumps is ample to throw a score of streams over the highest structures in the city; practically, the insufficient distribution of large mains renders this impossible in many localities.

— - —

POLICE SERVICE.

— —

FOR purposes of police patrol the City is divided into three districts, each having its police station and detachment of men. The headquarters of the Department are at the City Hall. The force consists of eighty-two men, including officers and detectives. Eight policemen are mounted, and patrol the outlying portions of the City, including the environs of Lakes Calhoun and Harriet and the Falls of Minnehaha.

A patrol wagon is provided, which will respond to calls by messenger or telephone at any hour. The Department also answers to the fire-alarm telegraph.

Considering the large area of the City and the limited number of men employed, the force does efficient service, but the beats assigned to the several patrolmen are too long, and, in view of the increasing density of the population, the City will be soon compelled to take action looking to a considerable enlargement of the force.

SANITARY SYSTEM.

THE deleterious influences which usually accompany the upbuilding and rapid peopling of a great City, and prejudice the physical well-being of its inhabitants, have, as yet, done little in Minneapolis to mar the natural healthfulness of the Minnesota climate. Nature has bestowed upon the place, in common with the greater portion of the State, a fine, dry, bracing atmosphere, which has acquired a wide reputation as a panacea for many diseases of the throat and chest.

Consumptives, in particular, attracted by the climate, come to the City in large numbers,—many to make good recoveries, and many others, resorting to the change at too late a stage of the disease to receive benefit therefrom, come only to die, and by their death help to swell the aggregate of mortality. Not less than six per cent. of the entire City death-rate is made up of this class.

Impure water, largely obtained from surface wells, and imperfect sewerage, have been instrumental in the production of an occasional epidemic, notably that of typhoid fever in 1881 and 1882, to which two-fifths of the annual number of deaths from this cause, reported below, must be referred. With the rapid extension of an improved system of sewers, the abandonment of surface wells, and the higher grade of intelligence concerning health-conditions, which is beginning to pervade this and other large communities, the probability of the outbreak of fresh epidemics of any character will be constantly lessened.

In a climate so nearly perfect as that of Minnesota, the assumption by any ordinary disease of an epidemic form, is distinctly chargeable upon the local government in the neglect of scavengering, sewerage or water-supply, or upon the uncleanly habits of large classes of people.

The improved condition of Minneapolis in these respects may be estimated from the fact that during the closing seven months of the year, covered by the health officer's last report, the death-rate per 1,000 per annum has declined from 29.40 to 12.42.

The average death-rate for the twelve months, ending March 1883, was 18.8 per 1,000, upon the health officer's estimate of a population of 80,000. More recent and more correct information places the population at over 94,000, which would reduce the death-rate to about 16.5.

Accepting the official estimate, the rate compares very favorably with that of other large cities of the continent.

The total of deaths for the year mentioned was 1,510. Of these 990 were of native, and 520 of foreign birth.

The following table is instructive as to the part which the several diseases play in making up this total number:

```
Deaths from Typhoid fever..................................................  164
   "      "   Consumption..................................................  135
   "      "   Diphtheria...................................................  117
   "      "   Pneumonia....................................................  109
   "      "   Accident.....................................................   51
   "      "   Scarlet fever................................................   24
   "      "   Measles......................................................   18
   "      "   Other diseases...............................................  895
                                                                          -----
                                                                           1510
```

HOSPITALS OF THE CITY.

O provision has yet been made for the public maintenance of a hospital by the City or County government, with the exception of the house provided for the seclusion and care of sufferers from small-pox.

Considering this fact, the accommodations for the sick, supported by private enterprise and voluntary contributions, are ordinarily good. Although they cannot, in all respects, fill the place of a well organized public institution, they are instrumental in supplying the most pressing needs of the very large community to which they minister in a fairly satisfactory and successful manner.

The hospitals are five in number. The largest among them, at the present time, is the corporation known as

THE MINNESOTA COLLEGE HOSPITAL. It is situated on the East side of the river, occupying a fairly commodious building, with a capacity of three hundred beds. It is in charge of an able corps of physicians, and nurses under the general direction of a board of trustees.

Minnesota College Hospital.

THE HOMŒOPATHIC HOSPITAL has been recently organized, and is now in working order. It has temporary quarters at the corner of Ninth Street and Eighth Avenue South, and can accommodate some fifty patients. Attached to it is a department called the *Hahnemann Ward*, supported by ladies of the City, and in charge of female physicians. This ward contains, at present, ten beds. The main hospital is under the care of competent homœopathic physicians. Those interested have purchased a building lot, upon which they purpose to erect, in due time, a permanent hospital.

THE SISTERS' HOSPITAL, situate at 2416 Sixth Street, South, is under the management of the Sisters of Mercy, who appoint the attending medical staff.

It can provide room for seventy-five patients.

THE ST. BARNABAS, OR COTTAGE HOSPITAL, on the corner of Sixth Street and Ninth Avenue, South, has facilities for the care of fifty patients.

It is under the management of the Brotherhood of Gethsemane.

THE NORTHWESTERN HOSPITAL, at present stands on Fourth Avenue, South, near Twenty-fourth Street, but will shortly remove to a building on Washington Avenue, North.

It has about fifteen beds for the use of the sick.

Each of these hospitals receives patients from the City, under orders from the Superintendent of the Poor. During the last year 377 persons were thus cared for and treated by the City Physician.

BENEVOLENT INSTITUTIONS.

IT may be said of the societies organized in Minneapolis for benevolent purposes that their "name is legion," and their work of the most varied character.

Although exhibiting greater or less degrees of excellence, they have, as a whole, contributed very largely to the well-being of the community, and especially to the improvement of the social condition of the laboring and distressed classes.

As a branch of the City Government, and a well-organized and valuable means of charity, the Department for the Poor, under care of the Superintendent, Mr. Nelson Williams, is deserving of special mention.

During the year, ending February, 1883, 3,905 applications for relief were answered, and 1,845 visits made by the Superintendent. Measures for relief were instituted in all deserving cases, at a cost of $18,140.58.

The following is a directory, in brief, of the principal benevolent organizations in the City, whose different branches of work it is impossible to review, in even the briefest manner, with justice to their ends and aims:

YOUNG MEN'S CHRISTIAN ASSOCIATION.—H. E. Fletcher, President; 519 and 521 Nicollet Avenue, and branch at Market Hall.

WOMAN'S CHRISTIAN TEMPERANCE UNION, and its auxiliary society, *The Young Woman's Christian Temperance Union,* 251 Nicollet Avenue.

SISTERHOOD OF BETHANY.—Mrs. VanCleve, President.

CATHOLIC ORPHAN ASYLUM.—Superintendent, Mother Mary James; 3rd Street, corner 6th Avenue, North.

CHILDREN'S HOME.—Matron, Miss Ellen I. V. Stewart; 22nd Avenue South, corner 6th Street.

HUMANE SOCIETY.—President, George A. Brackett.

WOMAN'S HOME.—President, Mrs. A. T. Hale; 409 South 6th St.

HEBREW RELIEF ASSOCIATION. - Secretary, Max Segelbaum.

MINNEAPOLIS FREE DISPENSARY.—President, C. A. Pillsbury; 208 South 2nd Street.

MINNEAPOLIS IRISH RELIEF ASSOCIATION.—President, Anthony Kelly.

IMMACULATE CONCEPTION, No. 349, I. C. B. U., 3rd Street, corner 3rd Avenue, North.

LADIES' HEBREW BENEVOLENT SOCIETY,—President, Mrs. R. Rees.

FIREMAN'S RELIEF ASSOCIATION.—President, F. L. Stetson.

CHARITY KINDERGARTEN.—President, Mrs. E. Morse.

BROTHERHOOD OF GETHSEMANE.—5th Street, corner 7th Avenue, South.

FATHER MATTHEW'S TEMPERANCE SOCIETY.—Catholic Association Hall.

CHURCHES.

T is an indication of the rapid growth of the city, as well as of the success of the Churches in their ordained work, that these organizations undergo a marked and regular increase in numbers. The large attendance at the Sunday services, the consequently enforced enlargement of many old buildings, or the erection of new, are witnesses to the interest and enterprise of the membership of these societies.

The churches and missions now established in Minneapolis number 76, and belong to 16 different denominations, as shown in the following table:

CHURCHES AND MISSIONS OF MINNEAPOLIS.

DENOMINATION.	No.
Advent	2
Baptist	9
Catholic (Roman)	7
Congregational	9
Christian	1
Disciples	1
Episcopalian	4
Evangelical Association	2
Evangelical Synod	1
Friends	1
Hebrew	1
Lutheran	4
"　　(German	2
"　　(Scandinavian)	8
Methodist Episcopal	14
Presbyterian	7
Swedenborgian	1
Unitarian	2
Universalist	1
Total	76

EDUCATIONAL INSTITUTIONS.

THE STATE UNIVERSITY.

THE UNIVERSITY OF MINNESOTA, situated upon the East side of Minneapolis, is a strong element in determining the present and future greatness of the City, and naturally occupies the foremost place in the history of her educational institutions.

The university was organized under a charter, enacted by the State Legislature, February 18th, 1868.

A grant of public lands was made by Congress for the endowment of the University, together with the department Colleges of Mechanics and Agriculture.

The lands thus granted to the institution have been partially sold, and will realize, when their sale is completed, over a million dollars.

The current expenses of the university are principally defrayed by the State.

A Board of Regents, ten in number, constitutes the governing body. This Board consists of, *ex-officiis*, the Governor of the State, the State Superintendent of Public Instruction, and the President of the University, together with seven others, appointed by the Governor, for a term of three years. •

7

The following persons are the members of the present board:

Hon. John B. Gilfillan, Minneapolis, Recording-Secretary.

Hon. Knute Nelson, Alexandria.

Hon. John S. Pillsbury, Minneapolis.

Hon. Henry H. Sibley, St. Paul, President.

Hon. Thomas S. Buckham, Faribault.

Hon. Greenleaf Clark, St. Paul.

Hon. Cushman K. Davis, St. Paul.

The Governor of the State, Hon. Lucius F. Hubbard, St. Paul ; The State Superintendent of Public Instruction, Hon. D. L. Kiehle, St. Paul ; and The Acting President of the University, William W. Folwell, Corresponding Secretary, *Ex-officiis.*

R. A. Davidson, Esq., President of the Commercial Bank of Minneapolis, is the treasurer.

The general Faculty, appointed by the Board of Regents, to undertake the management and instruction of students, consists of the following professors, instructors and assistants:

FACULTY OF THE STATE UNIVERSITY.

William W. Folwell, Instructor. Political Science. (Acting President.)

Jabez Brooks, D. D., Professor. Greek, and in charge of Latin.

Newton H. Winchell, Professor. State Geologist.

Chas. N. Hewitt, M. D., Non-resident Professor. Public Health and Hygiene.

John G. Moore, Professor. German.

Christopher W. Hall, Professor. Geology, Mineralogy and Biology.

John C. Hutchinson, Assistant Professor. Greek and Mathematics.

John S. Clark, Assistant Professor. Latin.

Matilda J. Wilkin, Instructor. German and English.

Maria L. Sandford, Professor. Rhetoric and Elocution.

William A. Pike. C. E. Professor. Engineering, and in charge of Physics.

John F. Downey, Professor. Mathematics and Astronomy.

James A. Dodge, Ph. D., Professor. Chemistry.

Charles W. Benton, Professor. French.

Edward D. Porter, Professor. Agriculture.

William H. Lieb, Instructor. Vocal Music.

Wilber F. Decker, B. M. E., Instructor. Physics, Shop Work, and Drawing.

William A. Noyes, Ph. D., Instructor. Chemistry.

FACULTY OF THE COLLEGE OF MEDICINE.

The recent lamented death of Professor Moses, Ph. D., and the resignation of Professor A. T. Ormond and E. C. Bower, U. S. A., leave vacancies in the chair of English, Mental and Moral Philosophy and History, and Miliary Science, which are, as yet, unfilled.

THE COLLEGE OF MEDICINE. — Within a few months, a department *College of Medicine* has been organized. Its faculty is to consist of nine professorships, and the following named gentlemen have been chosen to fill a part of these: The remaining three positions will soon be filled.

Dr. Charles N. Hewitt, of Red Wing, Professor of Preventive Medicine.

Dr. Franklin Staples, of Winona, Professor of the Practice of Medicine.

Dr. D. W. Hand, of St. Paul, Professor of Surgery.

Dr. W. H. Leonard, of Minneapolis, Professor of Obstetrics.

Dr. S. Millard, of Stillwater, Professor of Anatomy.

The present purpose of this College is not to give instruction in medicine and surgery. Its faculty will simply conduct examinations in these studies, and is empowered to confer the degree of *Doctor of Medicine* upon candidates who satisfactorily pass its examinations. Under an act of the Legislature of 1883, this faculty is constituted the State Examining Board, which is required to pass upon the qualifications of every practitioner of medicine in the State.

RECORDS OF ATTENDANCE.

The total number of students in attendance at the University during the year 1882, was 547. Of this number 253, or 178 gentlemen and 72 ladies, were enrolled in the classes of the general course; 192 persons attended the *Farmer's Lecture Course* given in January and February of each year for the purpose of instructing farmers in scientific agriculture; 52 mechanics studied at the *Free Evening Drawing School*, under the care of the Professor of Engineering and his assistants; 42 persons, principally teachers, attended the *Summer School*; and nine studied, under the private care of the Faculty, for the master's degree.

THE SUMMER SCHOOL, mentioned above, has been conducted annually for the past three years. It is intended for the convenience of teachers and others who cannot attend the regular sessions of the University, and its course of instruction, given gratuitously, have been, in the main, scientific. Modern languages, pedagogics, and, during the present summer, Greek, have also been studied with satisfactory results.

UNIVERSITY BUILDINGS, OUTFIT, ETC.

The present plant of the University has long been inadequate to the supply of recognized needs for space, but enlargement has, until now been impracticable.

A portion of an appropriation of $180,000, made by the State Legislature in 1881, becomes available during the present year, and as fast as it can be obtained, the Board of Regents will proceed to the erection of a gymnasium, military building, farm-house, museum, library, observatory, a separate building for engineering, chemistry and physics, a chapel, and a music-hall. When other plans are executed, the University will have room and equipment unequalled in the West.

The main building has, at present, fifty-four rooms. On its first floor is the University Library, the largest and most valuable in the State, numbering over 15,000 volumes. A reading room is in connection with the library for the accommodation both of the students and of the public.

On the third floor is the Museum, containing valuable collections of zoological, geological, and mineralogical specimens. One central case contains some of the minerals, building-stones, ore, clays, etc., of Minnesota.

The Geological Survey, made under the auspices of the Board of Regents, has contributed largely to these collections.

The Agricultural College Building contains the chemical laboratory, plant house, vice, forge, and woodshops, but is very much crowded in the attempted accommodation of these.

Students do not reside within the buildings.

A single charge of $5.00 a year is made to defray incidental expenses, but all instruction in every department is FREE.

The University has made great and rapid progress in its development, and, will ere long realize its ultimate plan of a system of department colleges under special management.

With the continued support of the people, and the maintenance of a superior class of instructors, it must soon take its place in the front rank of American Colleges, and may hope to surpass many of its sister institutions.

THE PUBLIC SCHOOLS.

The influences most active in shaping the public as well as the private life of a community, are those which emanate from the common school, and hence the character and condition of the latter may be looked to as important factors in the welfare of the home and of society. Their success or failure is a matter of vital interest to every citizen as well as to every prospective resident; and, in a city of so rapid a growth as Minneapolis, the maintenance of a high standard of public instruction, and the successful management of a large number of

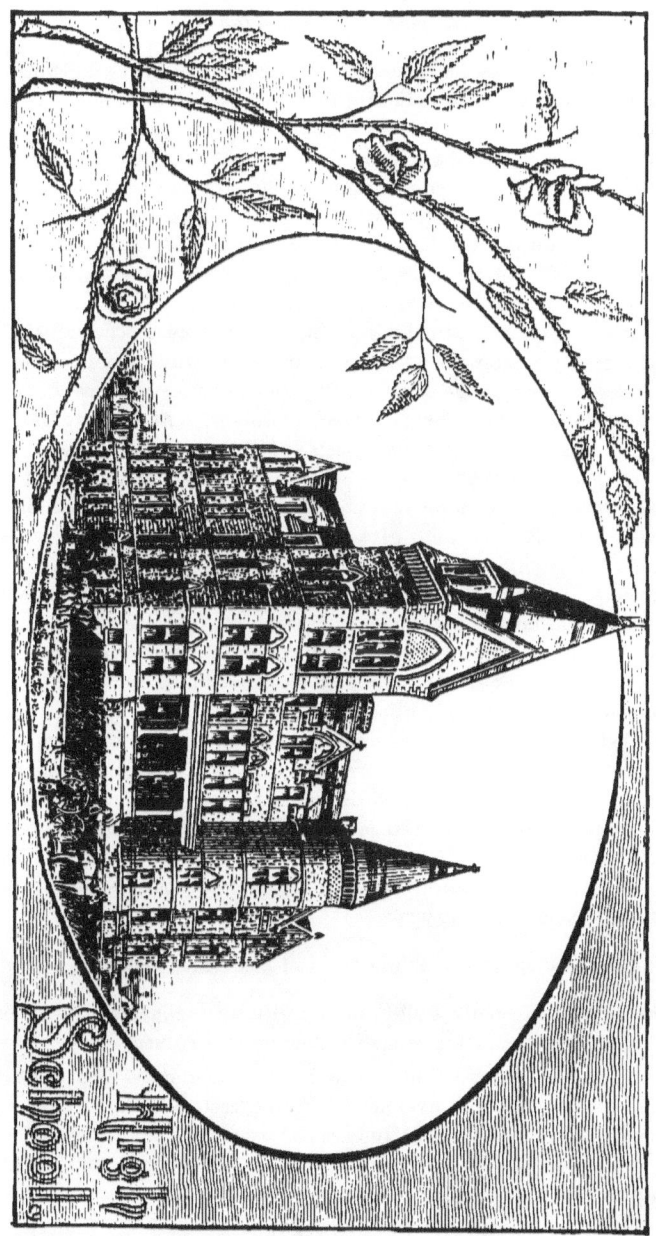

schools, are tasks beset with something more than ordinary difficulty.   It is due to the energy and public-spirit of the men who form the City School Board, as well as to the efficiency of the corps of principal instructors engaged by them, that the schools of Minneapolis can furnish, despite of the embarrassment of over-crowding, so good a record.   The city has twenty-two school buildings, with a total of 172 rooms.   Four of these schools were built during the last year at a cost of $100,000.   During the school year ending June, 1883, 10,698 pupils were admitted, an increase in number of 2,948 over the preceding twelve months.   The Board employs 215 teachers, including principals, at the present time.   The value of the school property is estimated at over $600,000.   Last winter the Board organized under the care of the Assistant Superintendent, a system of *Evening Schools* in three of the principal school buildings.   At the beginning of the year 1883, 934 pupils had been enrolled, with an average of 18 years of age.   These were under the care and instruction of a special corps of thirteen teachers, and were taught, mainly, in the elements of English studies.   Oral lessons were given upon practical topics with excellent results.   These schools are designed for those of school age, or over, who are unable to attend the ordinary day sessions, and yet are anxious to acquire the rudiments of a school education.

The constant influx of people to the city, and, in consequence, of children to the Public Schools, has long been a source of embarrassment.   Notwithstanding the recent additions, more new buildings are imperatively demanded, and some provision must be speedily made for them.   The standard of education will compare very favorably with that maintained in other large city schools, and the general record of advancement made by the pupils is above the average of available comparative reports.   With a better provision for over-crowded school districts, the grade of scholarship will probably be still higher, and the public school system of Minneapolis may be, at least, unsurpassed.

PRIVATE SCHOOLS AND SEMINARIES.

The city is unusually well-furnished with private institutions of learning, of which we cannot give more than a very brief mention:—

THE CURTISS BUSINESS COLLEGE, under the management of C. C. Curtiss, at the corner of Nicollet Avenue and Fifth Street, is an institution which has enjoyed a large degree of success and exercises a wholesome influence over the community.   Its classes are filled by young women as well as young men, and its total of persons in attendance, is between 400 and 500 annually.   Its aim is to furnish to its pupils a complete business education, and its success is a sufficient witness to its merit.

THE MINNEAPOLIS ACADEMY is a preparatory school to the State University, situated at 1328 Fourth St., S. E., and in charge of Mr. C. Davison.

BENNET SEMINARY is an excellent school for young ladies, in charge of Misses Kenyon and Abbott. It is situated at the corner of Tenth St. and Seventh Avenue south.

AUGSBURG SEMINARY is a Scandinavian school, which offers a high standard of training to its students. It stands on the corner of Seventh St. and Twenty-First Ave., south.

JUDSON FEMALE SEMINARY, conducted by Miss A. A. Judson, is another excellente stablishment for young ladies, at 44 Sixth St. south.

In addition to these the city has three medical schools, seven Catholic parochial schools and convents, two schools under Episcopalian management, three under different societies of the Lutheran Church, and three Kindergarten establishments, the latter constantly growing in public favor.

NEWSPAPERS AND PERIODICALS.

THE journalism of Minneapolis is represented by three daily newspapers, eighteen weeklies and nine monthlies.

The tendency in the daily journalism of the city has been toward a limited number of first-class, enterprising and well-supported papers rather than a multiplication of issues of inferior character, small circulation and trifling influence.

The Daily Minnesota Tribune, the only morning paper of the city, is a metropolitan journal of the first-class, having eight pages of the size and form of the New York Times and Chicago Tribune. Established only in 1880, it has promptly taken its place in the front rank of great American dailies, and its enterprise, ability and elevation of tone, have given it merited influence throughout the Northwest. It also maintains in the neighboring city of St. Paul a numerous corps of editors, reporters and business employes, and has a large circulation in that city, as well as over its entire field from central Wisconsin to the Rocky Mountains. The Tribune employs special representatives in Milwaukee, Chicago, New York, Washington and London, and has a special local correspondent in every important city and town in the Northwest. The proprietors have entered upon the enterprise of erecting a Tribune building, to occupy the northeast corner of Fourth Street and First Avenue, South, to be six stories in height, fire proof, to embody all the best architectural features of modern newspaper publishing offices, and to be equipped with the latest and fastest presses.

The Evening Journal, the oldest afternoon paper of the city, and the leading one in the State, was founded in 1880, and has attained a marked degree of success and large circulation. It also maintains a St. Paul department, and covers the two cities with its circulation. It has the exclusive use of the afternoon Associated Press dispatches for Minneapolis.

The Evening News, started in 1883, is a bright and enterprising journal more strictly local in its scope and purpose. It uses the dispatches of the United Press Association.

The Daily Pioneer Press and the Daily Globe, of St. Paul, respectively maintain editorial and business offices in Minneapolis and have a circulation in this city.

LIST OF WEEKLY PAPERS.

Farmers Union and Weekly Tribune.
Saturday Spectator.
Hennepin County Mirror.
Mississippi Valley Lumberman and Manufacturer.
Temperance Review.
Minneapolis Weekly.
Northwestern Miller.
Tourist and Sportsman.
Celtic World.
Freie Presse.
The Free Baptist.
Sunday Morning Call.
Svenska Folkets Tidning.
Unsi Kotimaa.
Budstikken.
Folkebladet
Canadian American.
Democrat.

MONTHLIES.

The Housekeeper.
The Homestead.
The Minnesota Farmer.
The Wood and Iron.
Minnesota Journal of Education.
Monthly Tourist and Sportsman.
Bibelbudet.
Mechanical World.

LIBRARIES.

THE origin of the only Library Association that Minneapolis possesses, dates back to the beginning of the year 1860, when "*The Minneapolis Athenæum*" was organized. Its history, up to the present date, has been one of steady development in the line of its original purpose. Starting with less than 300 books at its birth, it now catalogues over 14,000 volumes, covering every department of literature and science, and affording an invaluable resource to the general or special student. It maintains a reading-room, furnished with the best periodicals, and in which any book contained in the Library can be read or referred to, free of charge. Certain reference books are only used in this manner, no removal of them being permitted.

The general catalogue is open to transient or regular subscribers at all times. Upon deposit of $2.00, any book can be taken from the Library and retained for two weeks at a trifling fee per diem. Subscribers are allowed the use of two books at one time, at an annual rate. The Library is in charge of a Librarian and assistant, appointed by the officers and Directors of the Association. The rooms of the Association are at 217 Hennepin Avenue.

The library of 15,000 volumes attached to the State University has been already alluded to. This, through the medium of a reading-room, is open to the general public. It is the largest collection of volumes in the State.

The city has need of more extensive library advantages, and it is to be hoped that the organization of a Minneapolis Public Library is an event of the near future.

SCIENCE.

THE MINNESOTA ACADEMY OF NATURAL SCIENCE is the only association of the kind in Minneapolis. It was organized in 1873 and has maintained a prosperous existence ever since. Its object, in common with that of similar institutions in the United States, is "to observe and investigate natural phenomena; to make collections of specimens illustrating the various departments of science; to name, classify, and preserve the same; and to discuss such questions as shall come within the province of the Academy."

The rooms of the Academy are at 110 Hennepin Avenue, upstairs, in what is known as Kelly's block.

During the year the Academy holds monthly meetings, occurring on the Tuesday following the first Monday in the month. Its membership is about one hundred and fifty. Its officers are; A. F. Elliott, president; W. E. Leonard, vice-president; C. W. Hall, secretary; and N. H. Hemiup, treasurer, with a Board of nine Trustees. The bulletins of the Academy have been published annually and now form two printed volumes. The bulletin for 1882 is now in press. The collections and library are in the rooms of the Academy, at the above address.

MUSIC AND MUSICAL SOCIETIES.

THE recent May Festival, in Minneapolis, under the leadership of Theodore Thomas, with its home chorus of two hundred voices, attests the possibilities which careful training of the latent musical talent of the city may realize, and opens up to the city a future for the cultivation of music which will eventually place it on a par with the chief musical centres of the United States. The one great obstacle to negotiations for the visits of great musical artists, as well as to the maturing of home choral talent, is the lack of any building suited to concert purposes.

The musical organization, among those existing in Minneapolis, which possesses the highest order of musical power and gives evidence of the most thorough discipline and training, in the mastery of a high grade of music, is *Danz's Military Band and Orchestra.*

Among choral societies, *The Mendelssohn Club*—with its auxiliary, *The Madrigal Chorus*—occupies the first place. *The Club* consists entirely of male voices, whilst *The Chorus* is of mixed character. *The Apollo Club* is a male quartette of some local celebrity. *The Harmonia* and *Frohsin Societies* are under German management. One Norwegian and two Swedish societies complete the number of organized musical bodies. Special attention is paid to the teaching of music in the common schools, and private as well as public instruction in the city is carried to an unusually advanced stage.

WATERING PLACES

Summer Resorts

NEAR MINNEAPOLIS.

LARGE numbers of the residents of almost every American City are annually compelled by the unfortunate demands of failing health, over-wrought nervous systems, or prevailing fashion, to seek a change of scene or climate in some pleasure-resort or watering-place, at a distance from their homes.

The citizens of Minneapolis, however, are fortunately relieved from this oftentimes disagreeable necessity by the existence, in the immediate vicinity of the City, of a system of lakes beautifully adapted to every purpose of health, ease and pleasure. A single half-hour's journey will suffice to bring them within reach of all the material advantages possible to an inland watering-place, combined with the one absolutely essential element of a healthful and invigorating summer climate.

LAKES CALHOUN, HARRIET AND MINNETONKA.

The nearest of these to the center of the City are *Lakes Calhoun* and *Harriet*, embraced within the City limits. These are both small but beautiful pieces of water, less than a mile apart, with regular, sloping, wooded shores, and sand and gravel beaches, affording ample and commodious camping grounds.

LAKE CALHOUN, however, although visited daily by large numbers of people, is not much occupied for camping purposes, partly owing to the lack of that seclusion which is found elsewhere, and partly to its present depopulation of fish.

Its most prominent feature is the Lyndale Hotel, which, after being largely rebuilt and extended, has been reopened the present season, and is now an attractive residence for summer guests.

LAKE HARRIET has a larger supply of fish, and is surrounded by a number of cottages, and a small colony of camps.

LAKE MINNETONKA.—Far surpassing these smaller lakes in extent and beauty, and of far greater importance to the City, is the favorite summer resort of the Northwest, *Lake Minnetonka*.

This beautiful lake may be accounted as practically a suburb of Minneapolis, lying, as it does, only fifteen miles to the southwest, and supported, as it mainly is, by Minneapolis citizens.

Its greatest length is eighteen miles, and its width from one to five miles. It is divided into two main portions, the Upper and the Lower Lakes, linked together by a slender channel, called the Narrows. Its shore-line is remarkably indented, forming a series of picturesque bays, and having an estimated length of nearly three hundred miles.

A rich forest growth approaches, throughout the greater part of its extent, to the shore-line, and lends a new element of beauty to its varied scenery. Here and there upon the banks, small villages have sprung up, whose growth has been fostered by the erection of summer cottages and large hotels in their near neighborhood. These villages will be further noticed in detail.

A large number of cottages and villas, dotting the shores or the Lake, have been built and are occupied by citizens, not only of Minneapolis, but of many neighboring States. Their artistic forms, and bright, harmonious colors, add to the beauty with which nature has so richly endowed the place.

Even more numerous, and not less picturesque in their effect, are the white spots of canvas which mark the tents of transient or less permanent visitors, who realize, in the most approved manner, the merits of camp-life.

A majority of summer visitants from points outside Minnesota are annually quartered at the many hotels, where have sprung up at various points, to meet the demands of custom, and the location of which will be further noted.

A HEALTH RESORT.

Many of these visitors come to Minnetonka from all parts of the country in search of renewed health, and there are few places in America which can boast of more favorable conditions for their encouragement. All that climate can do for the majority of these cases of impaired vitality, in the many forms, may be expected of the air of Minnesota, under conditions so favorable to its energyzing influence, as may be obtained, at will, in the out-of-door life possible at Lake Minnetonka.

Hotel Lafayette, Lake Minnetonka.

Sufferers, especially from throat and chest diseases *in their earlier stages of development*, will realize the remarkable benefits to be obtained from the dry, bracing quality of the atmosphere, aided by the improved hygiene of tent-living.

VIEW OF WAYZATA.

The proximity of Minneapolis makes it possible to combine the com-forts and conveniences of City life with the advantages peculiar to the country. The railroads connecting with the Lake villages provide for the transmission of materials, and the local dealers supply dairy products and vegetables, of excellent quality, direct from the neighboring farms, delivering the same at the tents or cottages at ruling and reasonable prices.

Grounds for camping purposes, together with tent materials, are leased by the owners upon reasonable terms.

LAKE VILLAGES.

The principal villages situated on the banks of Minnetonka are, Excelsior, Wayzata, and Mound City.

LAKE PARK HOTEL.

EXCELSIOR was one of the earliest settlements in the State, having been colonized in 1852 and incorporated in 1879. It rests upon the south shore of the Lake, about eighteen miles from the City. It is reached by the Minneapolis & St. Louis and the Minneapolis, Lyndale & Minnetonka Railroads, is a main terminus for the large Steamboats on the Lake, and has postal, telegraph and telephone communications with the City. It possesses good business, school and church advantages, some of the best hotels and boarding places, of medium size, on the Lake, and excellent camping grounds. It enjoys the distinction of being free from saloons.

WAYZATA is situated on the north side of the Lake, and is fifteen miles distant from the city. It is reached by the St. Paul, Minneapolis and Manitoba Railway.

Although but half the size of Excelsior, it is in some respects more popular; a fact due largely to the surrounding cluster of summer cottages, and the maintenance of a more active sporting and yachting interest.

The village has two good hotels, and communicates by mail, telegraph, and telephone with Minneapolis.

MOUND CITY is a little place situated upon the Upper Lake, of which it has a fine outlook. It is visited by the steamers, and has a post-office, hotel, etc.

THE PRINCIPAL HOTELS.

The principal hotels of Lake Minnetonka are so essentially a feature of the place, and add so much by their architectural beauty, to its natural attractions, that they are deserving of mention as matters of public interest.

THE LAKE PARK HOTEL lies about a mile to the north of Excelsior, upon what is known as the "Minnetonka Lake Park." The latter is, in itself, a beautiful peninsula, to which the towers and frontage of the hotel add grace of form and harmony of color.

The hotel, which is surrounded by several handsome summer cottages, is four stories in height, sixty feet wide and 400 feet long. It has ample accommodations for nearly 500 people.

The steamers stop at the Lake Park landing upon each regular trip.

THE HOTEL LAFAYETTE stands upon a peninsula known as "Minnetonka Beach." The view, of which it forms a picturesque part, and the equally fine prospect from its own towers, are among the most beautiful upon the Lake. The Hotel was built in 1882, and enlarged during the present season, by the St. Paul, Minneapolis & Manitoba Railway Company. It has now a frontage of 800 feet, a height of four stories, and a capacity for accommodating nearly 1,000 guests. The railroad has a station at the hotel, and the steamboats a dock, which they visit upon each regular trip.

THE HOTEL ST. LOUIS occupies an equally fine point of ground, and is only second to the Lake Park and the Lafayette in capacity. It is placed upon the southern shore of the Lake, in a retreating curve of land enclosing a large bay; and lies upon high wooded grounds. The roof of the building commands a wide and beautiful prospect. It has 300 feet of frontage, and a height of three stories. It can furnish nearly 200 rooms. The Minneapolis & St. Louis R. R. has a station within a short distance of the hotel, and the steamers find a ready approach to it.

HOTEL ST. LOUIS.

A number of smaller hotels enjoy a leading reputation as successful hostelries, but possess no special architectural features to draw attention to them.

8

LAKE STEAMBOATS.

Two large side-wheel steamers, one of smaller capacity, and six small propellers ply constantly about Lake Minnetonka. The larger boats make regular trips to all the main points upon the lake shore, and connect with the railroad trains at Excelsior and Wayzata. Several steamers run between the stations on the Lower Lake and the hotels on the Upper Lake for the accommodation of transient daily visitors. The small propellers can be chartered for special trips at the direction of the party employing them. *

The steamer "City of St. Louis" is a fine side-wheeler, carrying 800 passengers.

The steamer "Belle of Minnetonka" is built upon a similar plan, but is considerably larger, having a carrying capacity of 2,000.

Both of these boats have a restaurant in which meals are regularly served.

The round trip of the Lake is some thirty miles in length.

WHITE BEAR LAKE AND MINNEHAHA.

WHITE BEAR LAKE, situated on the line of the St. Paul and Duluth Railway, about twelve miles from Minneapolis, is a miniature of Lake Minnetonka of the most perfect order. It is improved, principally, by citizens of St. Paul, who have surrounded it with handsome summer cottages. It has two first-class hotels, a good business connection, and a few private boarding places.

It is probably destined to gain a wide reputation as the meeting-ground of an Assembly organized upon the plan of the far-famed Chatauqua Assembly, for which a large tract on the north shore of the Lake has been bought.

THE FALLS OF MINNEHAHA, the "laughing-water" of Longfellow's verse has won so wide a fame that anything more than a passing reference to its beauties is unnecessary.

The Falls are situated about six miles from the City Hall, and some two miles beyond the city limits, a little to the southeast of the city, and on the line of the Chicago, Milwaukee and St. Paul R. R. They are supplied by Minnehaha Creek, the outlet of Minnetonka and smaller lakes surrounding the south and southwestern portions of the city. They are fifty feet in height and the rocks over which the water falls have undergone a recession similar to that observed at the Falls of St. Anthony.

Always picturesque, they are peculiarly so in the winter season when the formation of ice about the cataract adds a stranger beauty to the scene than is ordinarily its own.

BOATING, FISHING, HUNTING, ETC.

IN a section of country so rich in lakes and rivers as the neighborhood of Minneapolis the opportunities of the sportsman are practically inexhaustible, and the field of his enjoyment is unusually large and varied.

BATHING is so ordinary a pleasure that it is altogether unnecessary to give any hints concerning its exercise.

At all the principal lakes, and especially at Minnetonka, bathing houses are kept for hire and in connection with the large hotels, and bathing suits can also be obtained. The beaches are generally well adapted to this purpose and the water is delightfully fresh and pure.

BOATING in all its forms is amply provided for upon the lakes. Fleets of sailing vessels and row-boats are kept for renting purposes at Wayzata, Excelsior, Mound City, and one or two minor points, upon Lake Minnetonka. The hotels at this and other resorts provide row-boats for the use of their guests.

Yachting is a very popular sport upon the neighboring waters, and a number of regattas are held during the season, at Minnetonka and White Bear.

A successful and enthusiastic canoe-club, with a membership, for the most part, of Minneapolis gentlemen, is maintained at Lake Minnetonka with headquarters at the club boat-house on Excelsior Beach.

Steamboating has been already referred to upon an earlier page. Excellent opportunities are afforded at Excelsior for the formation of private excursions in small parties, and moonlight excursions are of frequent occurrence during the summer weeks.

FISHING AND HUNTING are naturally allied topics and may be considered together.

The waters, streams and forests within easy reach of the cities of Minneapolis and St. Paul, afford ample sport to satisfy the most insatiable hunter or fisherman. Within a few hours ride of either city, almost any variety of game may be secured in the proper season, whilst the supply of fish shows no perceptible diminution, save in very limited waters, from year to year.

As especially concerning sportsmen who are resident or visiting in Minneapolis, the opportunities only of the immediate surroundings of the City will be mentioned.

There is hardly a lake or a stream within one or two hours ride that will not afford an excellent quality of fishing.

The best waters are undoubtedly those of Lake Minnetonka. If the fisherman is unfamiliar with its bays and inlets, his best course is to obtain the services of an experienced boatman who can direct his sport and relieve him of much of the drudgery of boating, stringing, etc. With this assistance, he will undoubtedly achieve much more satisfactory results than unaided he could possibly obtain.

Pickerel, black and rock bass, croppies and sun-fish, are the varieties to be met with at Minnetonka and in most of the neighboring lakes.

White Bear Lake also affords a large supply of wall-eyed pike.

The regular track of the steamboats must of course be avoided, and the preference given to the more sheltered bays and coves in outlying situations. Trolling is very successful in the capture of pickerel. Still fishing is accomplished with minnows and small frogs.

The woods surrounding the more sequestered portions of Lake Minnetonka abound with pheasants, rabbits and black and gray squirrels.   An occasional deer is shot during the winter season.

At the onset of cold weather, the bays of Minnetonka and the small lakes surrounding it will afford the best of water-fowl shooting. Large numbers of woodcock may be taken, in season, along the banks of the Minnetonka River above the junction at Fort Snelling. In the country to the north of White Bear Lake, duck may be found in abundance.

The railroads of Minnesota are accustomed to transport one hundred pounds weight of camp furnishings, with dogs, guns, tackle, other apparatus, and game, free of charge. The owners of live animals are expected to provide for their proper care

The following synopsis of the game laws of the State of Minnesota may be useful to the visiting sportsman:

THE GAME LAWS OF MINNESOTA.

The following are the dates to which the destruction of game and fish of various kinds is limited:—Woodcock, July 4th to November 1st; Quail (Partridge), Pinnated Grouse (Prairie Chicken), Ruffed Grouse (Pheasant), September 1st to December 1st; Elk and Deer, November 1st to December 15th; Water Fowl, September 1st to May 15th; Brook Trout, April 1st to October 1st; Harmless birds, their eggs, or nests may not be destroyed; Wild Pigeons, Blackbirds and game are not included among harmless birds.

Exportation of all game, except Pheasants, is forbidden.

The possession of game in hand or in transit beyond the prescribed season is competent evidence for conviction of a violation of the law

Anyone entering fields of growing crops with dogs or hunting implements, without permission of the owner, is liable to a penalty for trespass.

The spearing or capture of fish in any other way than with hook and line is absolutely prohibited, except in the waters of Lake Superior and the Mississippi, Minnesota and St. Croix rivers.

THIRTY·SECOND ANNUAL MEETING

OF THE

American Association for the Advancemet of Science,

AT MINNEAPOLIS, AUG. 15 TO 21, 1883.

SPECIAL INFORMATION FOR THE USE OF MEMBERS
OF THE ASSOCIATION.

THE Thirty-second Annual Meeting of the Association will commence at ten o'clock A. M., Wednesday, August 15th, 1883. The headquarters of the Association will be at the University of Minnesota; the hotel headquarters will be at the Nicollet House, on Washington avenue, between Nicollet and Hennepin avenues. The general sessions and the meetings of the Sections and Committees will be at the State University.

The retiring address of President J. W. Dawson will be given at the Westminster Church on Nicollet avenue, on Wednesday evening.

The Reception by the Local Committee will be held at the Nicollet House on Wednesday evening, after the address of President Dawson.

Post-office, telegraph and telephone facilities will be found at the main University building. Letters may be addressed to members after August 12th, at Minneapolis, *care of the* A. A. A. S., and they will be delivered from the office of the Local Committee at the University.

By the courtesy of the Western Union Telegraph Company, social and personal messages will be transmitted free for members during the session of the Association.

Each member will be given a numbered badge which he is expected to wear during the meeting. The members of the Local committee will have a distinguishing badge.

Hacks and omnibuses that bear the initials A. A. A. S., will carry members at reduced rates to and from the University, and between hotels and the depots.

A daily luncheon will be served by the Local Committee in a temporary building on the University campus. Tickets of admission to this will be obtained daily at the office of the Local Committee at the University, or at the door.

The annual meeting of the SOCIETY FOR THE PROMOTION OF AGRICULTURAL SCIENCE will be held in Minneapolis on August 13th and 14th, in the Agricultural College building, of the State University.

A special meeting of the CAMBRIDGE ENTOMOLOGICAL CLUB will be held in Minneapolis, at the Chapel of the University, at two P. M., on Tuesday, August 14th, to which meeting all members and other persons interested in entomology are invited.

Excursions will be made as follows:

To Minnetonka and return Saturday afternoon, August 18th. A lawn picnic will be served at the Lake Park Hotel.

If a party of 150, or more, desire to make an excursion to Winnipeg and return at one-half of regular fare, the St. Paul, Minneapolis & Manitoba railway will send a special train for their accommodation.

The following reduced rates will be charged to Members at the hotels of the city and vicinity:

Nicollet House, per day, $3.00; without dinner, $2.00. Meal tickets for members can be obtained at the rate of twenty-one meals for $12.50. This hotel will be very much crowded, but if notice be given of friends who will room together, a large number can be accommodated.

St. James Hotel, Washington avenue south, per full day, $2.00; without dinner, $1.50. Day board per week, $6.00 and rebate for dinner. Twenty-one meal tickets for $6.00.

National House, Washington avenue south, per full day, $2.00; without dinner, $1.50.

Clark House, corner Hennepin avenue and Fourth street, per full day, $2.00; without dinner, $1.50.

Bellevue House, Washington avenue north, per full day, $2.00; without dinner, $1.50.

Lake Park Hotel, at Lake Minnetonka, south side, $2.50 per day including dinner.

Hotel Lafayette, at Lake Minnetonka, north shore, $2.50 per day, including dinner at 6 p. m.

St. Louis Hotel, at Northome on Lake Minnetonka, east end, $2.50 per day, including dinner at 6 p. m.

White House, Excelsior, on Lake Minnetonka, $1.50 without dinner.

Lyndale Hotel, at Lake Calhoun, $2.50 per day, including dinner at 6 p. m.

Excelsior House, per full day, $2.50; without dinner, $1.50.

Members who attend will be favored with reduced railroad rates of travel, according to the following list. In order to obtain these privileges they must be supplied with certificates of membership from the Permanent Secretary:

Burlington, Cedar Rapids & Northern Railway.......Return members at one-fifth fare.
Baltimore & Ohio Railroad.............................Trunk line pool agreement.
Boston & Albany Railroad............................... "   "   "
Chicago & Northwestern Railway.....................Return members at one-fifth fare.
Chicago, Milwaukee & St Paul Railway.............. "   "   "
Chicago, St. Paul, Minneapolis & Omaha Railroad....   "   "   "
Chicago, Rock Island & Pacific Railroad............   "   "   "
Cleveland, Columbus, Cincinnati & Indianapolis R'y........Regular round trip tickets.
Chicago & Grand Trunk Railway......{ To Chicago and return at one and one-third fare on certificate.
Fitchburg Railroad...Trunk line agreement.
Grand Trunk Railway..................{ From any station to Chicago and return at one and one-third fare on certificate.
Illinois Central Railroad..................No reduction from regular round trip rates.
Indianapolis, Bloomington & Western R'y   "   "   "   "
Jeffersonville, Madison & Indianapolis R'y   "   "   "   "
Louisville, New Albany & Chicago R'y....   "   "   "   "
Louisville & Nashville Railway...........   "   "   "   "
Lake Superior Transit Company..No reduction.
Minneapolis & St. Louis Railway...........Return members at one-fifth on certificate.
Northern Pacific Railroad...........................Return members free on certificate.
New York Central Railroad..................................Trunk line agreement.
New York Lake Erie & Western...............{ One-third fare returning, unless less is made
Ohio & Mississippi Railway..................{ by competing lines.
Peoria, Decatur & Eastern Railroad.......Return members at one-third on certificate.
Pennsylvania Company (P., Ft. W. & C.)...Regular round trip rate to and from Chicago.
Rock Island & Peoria Railroad................{ Same as competing lines; return members at one-fifth fare.
St. Paul & Duluth Railroad.............Return at one fifth fare on certificate.
St. Louis & St. Paul Packet Company..........Return at one-third fare on certificate.
St. Paul, Minneapolis & Manitoba Railway........Return members free on certificate.

The railroads to lake Minnetonka will carry members, bearing their certificate, free, between Minneapolis and their stations on lakes Minnetonka and Calhoun.

The St. Paul, Minneapolis & Manitoba Railroad will leave members at Wayzata and at Hotel Lafayette.

The Minneapolis and St. Louis Railroad will carry members to the St. Louis Hotel and to the Lake Park Hotel, also to the hotels at Excelsior.

The Minneapolis, Lyndale & Minnetonka Railroad (narrow gauge) will bring members to the Lyndale Hotel at lake Calhoun, and the hotels at Excelsior.

These suburban hotels are about twelve miles from Minneapolis, and trains run frequently on all the roads, making the distance in about thirty minutes.

TIME TABLE OF TRAINS BETWEEN MINNEAPOLIS AND LAKES MINNETONKA AND CALHOUN.

ST. PAUL, MINNEAPOLIS & MANITOBA RAILROAD.
GOING WEST.

LEAVES AS FOLLOWS.	Except Sunday	Except Sunday	Every Day	Every Day	Every Day	Every Day	Every Day.	On Sat'day
	A. M.	A M.	A M.	P. M.	P. M.	P. M.	P M	P. M.
East Minneapolis	6.45	7.48	9.55	1.55	4.55	5.55	7.30	10.55
Minneapolis..........	6.50	7.55	10 00	2.00	5 00	6.00	7.40	11.00
Wayzata..	7 15	8.37	10.25	2.25	5.25	6.25	8.23	11.25
Hotel Lafayette	7 25		10.35	2.35	5.35	6 35		11.35
Spring Park.......	7.32		12 42	2.42	5 42	6.42 ·		11.42

GOING EAST.

LEAVES AS FOLLOWS.	Except Sunday	Except Sunday	Except Sunday	Every Day	Every Day	Every Day	Every Day	Tues. Thurs. and Sat.
	A M.	A.M.	A.M.	A M.	P.M.	P.M.	P M	P.M.
Spring Park.......................		6.45	7.45	8.45	12.45	4 45		10 35
Hotel Lafayette		6.55	7.55	8 55	12 55	4.55		10.45
Wayzata.....................	6.25	7.05	8.05	9 05	1.05	5.05	5.58	10.55
Minneapolis..........	7.00	7 30	8 30	9.30	1.30	5 30	6.30	11.20
East Minneapolis	7.05	7 35	8.35	9.35	1.35	5.35	6.35	11.25

MINNEAPOLIS & ST. LOUIS RAILWAY.
TO THE LAKE.

STATIONS.	Daily	Daily	Daily	Daily Except Sunday	Daily	Tuesday Wed. and Saturday
	A. M.	A. M.	A. M.	P. M.	P. M.	P. M.
Minneapolis.......... Leave	7.15	9.30	11 50	4.00	5.45	7.15
Minnetonka Mills.... "	7 50	10.00	PM12.20	4.35	6.15	7.45
Northome (Hotel St L) "	7.50	10.05	12.29	4.45	6.25	7.55
Fairview.............. "	8.05	10.15	12.35	....	6.30	8.00
Solberg's Point ...... "	8.09	10.19	12.39	4.55	6.34	8.04
Excelsior..... .... "	8.11	10.23	12.41	5.00	6.37	8 08
Park Junction....... "	8 14	10.27	12.44	....	6.40	8.11
Lake Park............Arrive	8.18	10.31	12.48	....	6.44	8.15

FROM THE LAKE.

STATIONS.	Daily	Daily Except Sunday	Daily	Daily	Daily	Tuesday Wed. and Saturday
	A. M.	A. M.	A. M.	P. M.	P. M.	P. M.
Lake Park............. Leave	7.05	....	8 45	2.50	5.28	10.45
Park Junction........ "	7.08	....	8.49	2.54	5.32	10.49
Excelsior............... "	7.12	10.30	8.53	2.58	5.36	10.53
Solberg's Point...... "	7.15	10.33	8.57	3.02	5.40	10.57
Fairview . .. . "	7.19		9.00	3.05	5.43	11.00
Northome (Hotel St L) "	....	10.38	9.05	3.10	5.48	11.05
Minnetonka Mills.... "	7.33	10.51	9.15	3.20	5.55	11.15
Minneapolis..........Arrive	8.02	11.35	9.45	3.55	6.28	11.45

MINNEAPOLIS, LYNDALE AND MINNETONKA RAILWAY.

GOING WEST.

STATIONS. LEAVE	A.M. Sunday Except	A.M. Sunday Except	A.M. Daily	A.M. Daily	A.M. Daily	A.M. Daily	A.M. Daily	P.M. Daily	P.M. Daily	P.M. Daily	P.M. Daily	P.M. Daily	P.M. Daily	P.M. Sunday Except	P.M. Sunday	P.M. Daily	P.M. Daily	P.M. Daily
MINNEAPOLIS	6.43	7.30	8.15	8.45	9.30	10.30	11.30	12.15	12.45	1.30	2.15	3.00	3.45	4.30	5.15	6.05	6.15	7.15	8.40	9.15	10.30	11.30
LAKE CALHOUN	7.15	8.00	9.15	9.15	9.30	10.00	11.00	11.30	12.37	1.15	2.00	2.45	3.30	4.15	5.00	5.40	6.35	7.15	8.40	9.15	10.30	11.30	12.00
LAKE HARRIET	8.18				10.03	11.05	11.45		1.29	2.16					5.45	6.40	7.20	8.30	9.18	10.05
EXCELSIOR	9.29	10.11						1.29	2.43	3.35	4.15	5.00	5.45				8.01	9.58

GOING EAST.

STATIONS. LEAVE	A.M. Sunday Except	A.M. Sunday Except	A.M. Daily	A.M. Daily	A.M. Daily	A.M. Daily	A.M. Daily	P.M. Daily	P.M. Daily	P.M. Daily	P.M. Daily	P.M. Daily	P.M. Daily	P.M. Sunday Except	P.M. Sunday	P.M. Daily	P.M. Daily	P.M. Daily
EXCELSIOR			7.30	8.07	9.50	9.50	11.20		1.25	1.35	2.30	3.05	3.40	4.30	5.10	6.10	6.40	7.10	7.50
LAKE HARRIET	6.05		8.07	10.30	10.30	11.40	12.00		1.25	2.30	3.05	3.49	5.15	5.10	6.10	6.45	7.25	8.55	10.15
LAKE CALHOUN	6.10	6.50	8.10	8.50	9.50	10.33	11.30	12.10	12.50	2.05	2.50	3.40	1.35	5.15	6.10	6.50	7.25	8.00	8.55	10.15
MINNEAPOLIS	6.40	7.30	8.35	9.15	10.20	11.03	11.55	12.40	1.20	1.30	2.50	3.40	1.18	5.10	6.10	7.20	7.50	8.30	9.20	10.15	11.22

ARRIVAL AND DEPARTURE OF TRAINS.
TIME TABLE.

CHICAGO, MILWAUKEE & ST. PAUL RAILWAY.
HASTINGS & DAKOTA DIVISION.

TRAIN.				TIME.
Arrives at Minneapolis from Aberdeen at				6:30 A. M.
"	"		"	6:25 P. M.
Leaves	"	for	"	7:00 A. M.
"	"	"	"	7:35 P. M.

IOWA & DAKOTA DIVISION.

TRAIN.				TIME.
Arrives at Minneapolis from Mitchell at				7:05 P. M.
Leaves	"	for	"	8:00 A. M.
"	"	"	"	6:00 P. M.

MAIN LINE RIVER, DIVISION.

Arrives at Minneapolis from Chicago at				7:00 A. M.
"	"	"	"	3:10 P. M.
Leaves	"	for	"	12:00 Noon.
"	"	"	"	7:00 P. M.

CHICAGO, ST. PAUL MINNEAPOLIS & OMAHA.
MAIN LINE.

TRAIN.				TIME.
Arrives at Minneapolis from Chicago at				7:00 A. M.
"	"	"	"	3:10 P. M.
Leaves	"	"	"	12:00 Noon.
"	"	"	"	7:00 P. M.

ST. PAUL & DULUTH RAILWAY.

TRAIN				TIME.
Arrives at Minneapolis from Duluth at				7:55 A. M.
"	"	"	"	5:45 P. M.
Leakes	"	for	" ·	8:10 A. M.
"	"	"	"	6:00 P. M.

ST. PAUL, MINNEAPOLIS & OMAHA RAILWAY.

TRAIN.	TIME.
Arrives at Minneapolis from Fargo, Grand Forks, and Brecken- ridge at.....................................	7:00 A. M.
Arrives at Minneapolis from Fargo, Grand Forks and Brecken- ridge at.....................................	6:45 P. M.
Leaves Minneapolis for Fargo, Grand Forks and Breckenridge at.....................................	8:00 A. M.
Leaves Minneapolis for Fargo, Grand Forks and Breckenridge at.....................................	7:45 P. M.
Arrives at Minneapolis from St. Vincent at..................	6:45 A. M.
" " " "	6:10 P. M.
Leaves " for "	8:45 A. M.
" " " "	9:30 P. M.

NORTHERN PACIFIC RAILWAY.

TRAIN	TRAIN.
Arrives at Minneapolis from Bismarck at..................	7:30 A. M.
Leaves " for "	9:10 P. M.
Arrives " from Portland, and New Tacoma via. Helena, Mandan, Bismarck and Fargo..............	7:00 P. M.
Leaves Minneapolis for Portland and New Tacoma via. the same...	9:25 P. M.

MINNEAPOLIS & ST. LOUIS RAILWAY.

TRAIN.	TIME.
Leaves Minneapolis for Chicago......................	7:40 A. M.
" " "	7:00 P. M.
" " St. Louis and Des Moines........	7:40 A. M.
" " " "	3:10 P. M.

MINNEAPOLIS & ST. PAUL.

SHORT LINE TIME TABLES.

CHICAGO, MILWUKEE & ST. PAUL.

† Via Minnehaha.
* Except Sunday.

EAST BOUND.

	a. m.		a. m.	a. m.	a. m.	a. m.	a. m.	a. m.	noon.	p. m.	p. m.	p. m.	p. m.	p. m.	p. m.	p. m.	p. m.	p. m.
Lv Minneapolis	*7.00		†*8.00	8.00	*9.00	10.50	11.00	*11.45	*12.00	1.00	2.00	3.00	4.00	†*4.30	5.10	6.00	*6.40	7.00
Ar St. Paul	7.30		9.10	8.30	9.30	10.30	11.30	12.15	12.31	1.31	2.30	3.30	4.30	5.23	5.30	6.30	7.10	7.30

WEST BOUND.

	a. m.	a. m.	a. m.	a. m.	a. m.	a. m.	a. m.	noon.	p. m.	p. m.	p. m.	p. m.	p. m.	p. m.	p. m.	p. m.	p. m.
Lv St. Paul	6.25	†7.00	*4.00	9.00	†*9.30	*10.00	11.00	*12.00	1.00	2.40	*2.40	3.00	4.00	5.00	†*5.50	6.00	7.00
Ar Minneapolis	7.00	7.30	8.30	9.50	10.35	10.30	11.30	12.30	1.30	2.30	3.10	3.30	4.31	5.35	7.05	6.30	7.30

ST. PAUL, MINNEAPOLIS & MANITOBA.

* Except Sunday.
§ Except Monday.

EAST BOUND.

	a. m.	a. m.	a. m.	a. m.	a. m.	a. m.	p. m.	p. m.	p. m.	p. m.	p. m.	p. m.	p. m.	p. m.	p. m.
Lv Minneapolis	7.00	*7.15	8.30	9.30	10.30	11.30	*12.00	12.30	1.30	*2.3.	3.30	4.30	*5.30	6.30	7.00
Ar St. Paul	7.30	7.45	9.00	10.00	11.00	12.00	12.90	1.00	2.00	3.00	4.00	5.00	6.00	7.20	7.30

WEST BOUND.

	a. m.	a. m.	a. m.	a. m.	a. m.	a. m.	a. m.	p. m.	p. m.	p. m.	p. m.	p. m.	p. m.	p. m.	p. m.	p. m.	p. m.	p. m.	p. m.
Lv St. Paul	§6.25	*7.15	*4.00	8.30	8.35	9.30	11.30	12.30	1.30	2.30	2.35	3.30	4.30	5.30	5.50	6.30	7.00	8.15	8.40
Ar Minneapolis	7.00	7.55	8.40	9.00	9.10	9.10	10.04	11.0	12.00	1.00	2.00	3.00	3.10	4.30	5.00	6.00	6.30	7.00	8.55	9.20

OFFICERS AND MEMBERS OF THE LOCAL COMMITTEE AND OF THE SUB-COMMITTEES.

GENERAL EXECUTIVE COMMITTEE.

Hon. G.A.Pillsbury, *Ch'r'n*,
Prof. N.H Winchell, *Sec'y*,
Hon. George A. Brackett.
Hon. A. C. Rand.
Hon. John De Laittre.
W. W. McNair, Esq.
Hon. John S. Pillsbury.
Dr. W. W. Folwell.
Mr. Charles W. Johnson.

Gen. A. B. Nettleton.
Hon. W. D. Washburn
Mr. T. B. Walker.
Hon. O. C. Merriman.
Hon Eugene M. Wilson.
Mr. E. V. White.
Mr. H. T. Welles.
Hon. H. G. Hicks.
Thomas Lowry, Esq.

Mr. Winthrop Young.
Hon. William S. King.
David Blakely, Esq.
Hon. R. B. Langdon.
Supt. D. L. Kiehle.
1. C. Seeley, Esq
Mr. Anthony Kelly.
Dr. A. F. Elliott.
Hon. F. W. Brooks.

COMMITTEE OF ALDERMEN FROM THE CITY COUNCIL.

M. W. Glenn, *Chairman*.
F. L. Greenleaf.

E. Eichhorn.
N H. Roberts.
Matthew Walsh.

E. M. Johnson.
S. P. Channell.

SUB-COMMITTEE ON INVITATION AND RECEPTION.

Dr.W.W.Folwell, *Chairman*.
Mr. D. C. Bell.
Hon. E. M. Wilson.
Mr. Samuel Hill.
Mr. C. M. Loring.
Hon. C. A. Pillsbury.
Hon. A. A. Ames, (Mayor.)
Hon. J. B. Gilfillan.
Rev. J. H. Tuttle.
Hon. H. G. Hicks.
Gen. A. B. Nettleton.
Rev. James McGolrick.
Bishop Cyrus D. Foss.
Mr. C. McC. Reeve.
Dr. George F. French.
Dr. C. L. Wells.
V. S. Ireys, Esq.
Rev. D. B. Knickerbacker.
Mr. R. E. Grimshaw.
Hon. A. C. Rand.
S. C. Gale, Esq.
W. W. McNair, Esq.
C. A. Van Anda, D. D.
Mr. O. A. Pray.
Judge C. E. Vanderburg.
Mr. B. F. Nelson.

Robert S. Innes, Esq.
Dr. H. H. Kimball
1. C. Seeley, Esq.
Mr. R. J. Mendenhall.
Mr. S. A. Harris.
Prof. S. Oftedal.
Dr. W. H. Leonard.
Mr. C. F. Hatch.
Mr. Fred Hooker.
Judge William Lochren
Hon D. Morrison.
Mr. N. F. Griswold.
Mr. J. W. Griffin.
Mr. T. B. Casy.
Rev. H. C Woods.
J. B. Atwater, Esq.
Mr. W. E. Burwell.
Mr. Winthrop Young.
Rev. Robert Forbes.
Mr. R. C. Benton.
Judge John P. Rea.
Rev. R. F. Sample.
Col. William McCrory.
Mr. G. A. Wheaton.
Mr. J. T. Elwell.
Mr. C. H. Prior.

Mr. T. F. Andrews.
Hon. R. B. Langdon.
Mr. J. N. Nind.
Hon. R. Chute.
Hr. George H. Christian.
R. G. Hutchins. D. D.
Judge A. H. Young.
Mr. George A. Camp.
Mr. Clinton Morrison.
Judge J. M. Shaw.
Capt. J. C. Whitney.
Hon. Loren Fletcher.
Mr. John Crosby.
Judge G. B. Cooley.
Mr. J. H. Clark.
Prof. Jabez Brooks.
Mr. W. H. Hinkle.
Capt. J. N. Cross.
Mr. G. H. Clinton.
Mr. A C. Loring.
Mr. C. W. Johnson.
Hon. O. C. Merriman.

LADIES' RECEPTION COMMITTEE.

Mrs.J.S.Pillsbury, *Ch'rm'n*.
Mrs. Richard Chute.
Miss Maria Sanford.
Mrs. N. H. Winchell.

Mrs. W. W. Folwell.
Mrs. J. B. Gilfillan.
Miss Addie Pillsbury.
Miss Emily McMillan.

Mrs. L. W. Campbell
Mrs. F C. Barrows.
Miss Lettie Crafts.
Miss Addie Camp.

SUB-COMMITTEE ON ROOMS AND PLACES OF MEETING.

Hon. E. M. Wilson, *Ch'rm'n*.
Hon. R. B. Langdon.

Mr. C. W. Johnson.
Mr. Anthony Kelly.
Dr. A. F. Elliott.

Hon C. M. Loring.
Prof. J. A. Dodge.

SUB-COMMITTEE ON ENTERTAINMENT, HOTELS, LUNCHEONS AND LODGINGS.

Hon. A. C. Rand, *Chairman*,
Mr. R. F. Jones.
Stephen Mahony, Esq.
Hon Geo. A. Brackett.
George H. Fletcher, Esq.
Dr. F. A. Dunsmoor.
Mr. T. B. Walker.
Col. R. S. Innes.

Dr. Charles Simpson.
Mr. W. M. Tenney.
Fred Lathrop, Esq.
Dr. A. W. Abbott.
Mr. Wesley Neil.
Mr. J. F. Collum.
T. E. Byrnes, Esq.
Prof. William J. Warren.

Dr. Charles R. Chute.
E. Chatfield. Esq.
Hon. D. L. Kiehle.
Prof. J. F. Downey.
Mr. C. C. Sturtevant.
Dr. P. L. Hatch.

SUB-COMMITTEE ON FINANCE.

I. C. Seeley, Esq., *Chairman*.
Mr. H. G. O. Morrison.
Mr. N. F. Griswold.
Mr. O. T. Swett.

J. W. Perkins, Esq.
Mr. S. B. Lovejoy.
Judge Francis Bailey.
Mr. Albert Hastings.
Hon. Josiah Thompson, Jr.

Frank H. Carleton, Esq.
Hon. H. T. Welles.
Mr. F. W. Brooks.
Mr. Isaac McNair.

SUB-COMMITTEE ON PRINTING AND ADVERTISING.

Mr. David Blakely, *Ch'rm'n.*
Mr. C. A. Nimocks

Gen. A. B. Nettleton.

Hon. W. S. King.
Prof. C. W. Hall.

SUB-COMMITTEE ON TRANSPORTATION AND EXCURSIONS.

Thos. Lowry, Esq., *Ch'rm'n.*
Hon. W. D. Washburn.
Maj. C. F. Hatch.
Mr. E. V. White.

Mr. John Crosby.
Mr. W. H. Hinkle.
Hon. J. S. Pillsbury.
Mr. Llewellyn Christian.
Hon. J. B. Bassett.

Mr. C. H. Prior.
Mr. A. H. Bode.
Mr. W. H. Truesdale.
Col. William McCrory.

www.ingramcontent.com/pod-product-compliance
Lightning Source LLC
Chambersburg PA
CBHW030907050726
47500CB00009B/1135